STARRING

Book Four of *The Drugstore Series*

ALSO BY SD SHELTON

Me, the Crazy Woman, and Breast Cancer

The Drugstore

The Life of Old Pete

Talking to Tubby

STARRING

DOLL DAHL

Book Four of *The Drugstore Series*

A NOVEL
by

SD SHELTON

ENLIGHTEN
PRESS

ENLIGHTEN PRESS
A DIVISION OF ENLIGHTEN COMMUNICATIONS, INC.

Enlighten Press

A Division of Enlighten Communications, Inc.
Norman, Oklahoma

Starring Doll Dahl
Book Four of The Drugstore Series

First Enlighten Press trade paperback edition September 2018

Manufactured in the United States of America

10 9 8 7 6 5 4 3 2 1

Paperback ISBN 978-0-9997297-1-7
EBook ISBN 978-0-9997297-0-0

Library of Congress Control Number: 2018955694

For more information about special discounts for bulk purchases, please contact Enlighten Press at enlightenpress@cox.net

For my mother-in-law,

Barbara Hibbs Shelton,

Whose love for all her daughters

Knows no boundaries.

"Perhaps

she will land

upon That Shore,

not in full sail,

but rather,

a bit of broken wreckage

for Him

to gather."

— Ruth Bell Graham

CHAPTER ONE

Trudy Dahl had always been beautiful. From the day she came out of her mother's womb she was nothing short of stunning. She had also been petite. She weighed only four pounds, nine ounces but immerged with beautiful blonde locks and the most intense blue eyes anyone had seen. Homozygous Blue they called them.

She hadn't really known what that meant until her sophomore biology class when she had studied genetics. Her teacher, Mr. Brewer, had made them fill out a chart with dominant and recessive gene eye colors. She remembered that brown was always dominant and blue eyes were recessive, but for some reason, she had come out a dominant blue. And although science wasn't her forte', it made some sense. Everyone in her family had blue eyes. However, hers were the bluest of them all.

Even though she lived in a small town in Oklahoma, where a large part of the population was Indian, the whole of her family also had blond hair. It was only natural because both her mother's and father's grandparents emigrated from Scandinavia. In fact, her own parents had been the first generation born in the United States, as her grandparents were children when the families made America their home.

Trudy's father, Knute, was Swedish and her mother, Elsa, was Norwegian. Both families had settled in Story County, Iowa and lived on the same block. Both of Trudy's great-grandfathers owned small businesses, which were only two doors apart from each other on the town square. Her father's grandfather was a chocolatier and her mother's grandfather was a baker. The two men became fast friends and remained so until they died.

Elsa and Knute's families continued operation of the businesses and remained very close through the ensuing generations. Indeed, neither Knute, nor Elsa, had ever remembered a time in their lives when they were without the other.

Trudy's father was two years older than her mother, but Knute and Elsa had been inseparable since they were toddlers. By the time the couple were in the third grade, they were in the same class because Knute, who was small and one of the youngest, was held back a year. Elsa, who could already read before she entered the first grade, was moved ahead. It was fine with the both of them, as each had never adjusted to being apart. It was also fine with the families because separating the two had caused significant problems.

On Knute's very first day of school, when it came time for him to leave, Elsa squalled like she was being beaten. Although her mother tried everything she could imagine, including ice cream for breakfast, there was nothing she could do to console the hysterical child. Elsa, wailed and repeatedly threw herself to the floor, kicking at everything in sight, until her mother scooped her up into her arms and rocked the distraught child while assuring her that Knute would be home soon. When the time came for Knute to arrive, with tears still flowing, her mother took her to the front porch so they could watch for his return. The second Elsa saw her beloved friend, she ripped herself from her mother's arms and ran to him, wrapping him in a hug from which she had to be pried.

"Why did you leave?" she screamed, tears streaming down her chubby and very red cheeks. "Neber, neber, leave me again!"

The following day, both mothers, along with the entwined children, walked together to Knute's school. When they arrived, Elsa was shown Knute's classroom. Thinking that if she understood where he was, it would ease her pain, they explained that Knute would be in his classroom five days of the week, but he would always come back to her.

Elsa wasn't having it. As soon as Knute's teacher began to close the classroom door on them, Elsa began her wailing. She screamed until her face exploded in a violent red and she jumped up and down like a wild animal. She ran to her mother, tugging at her dress and begging her to open the door. Elsa's mother picked up the child and scurried as quickly as possible outside. Knute's mother followed, trying to placate the child from behind. Once outside, the already hysterical girl, turned into a banshee, screaming so loudly that school children rushed to every window to see who was being maimed.

Elsa's mother sat her down and put her hands around the child's face.

"Elsa, you have to calm down. Knute isn't gone, he is right inside."

Elsa shook her head no and tried to speak through her blubbering.

"My Knute," she gasped. "Bwing him to me. Pwease Momma," she begged.

"If you will calm down, we will work something out, but not until you get control of yourself."

Elsa struggled for a breath between sobs, as she tried to calm herself.

"Good, that's better," he mother soothed as she led her daughter to the school's steps. She looked down at her heart-broken daughter.

"What if we wait right here for Knute to get out? Do you promise to stop crying if we do that?"

Elsa nodded, her blond curls bobbing. Then she planted her face in her mother's lap and quietly wept until her beloved companion was released.

Walking Knute to school and waiting on him continued for several days. After about a week, the headmaster, having pity on them, invited Elsa and her mother to stay in the library. Elsa's mother would read her books and let her work wooden puzzles, while she herself, knitted, darned, or attended to the accounting for their small store.

On sunny days, mother and child would sit on a blanket beneath the large oaks that adorned the campus of the small school. Elsa would hunt and identify insects, while her mother shelled peas, sewed together pieces of a quilt, or embroidered pillow cases. After a picnic lunch, Elsa would stretch out on the blanket and nap until her beloved Knute would once again emerge from what Elsa assumed was his prison.

When Elsa herself was finally able to attend school, Knute was her guardian. Wherever Elsa went, Knute was there. He defended her when the other children made fun of her lisp.

"Stop! You're just jealous because she's so pretty!" he shouted at taunting little girls, who would only momentarily obey.

Because Elsa was never left alone for more than a few days at a time, Knute planted himself next to her throughout their remaining grades school years, and made sure to arrange that they had the same classes when they moved on to junior high and high school.

By the time they made their transition into their teenage years, the two had basically become one. In fact, one's name was never mentioned without the other. It was during that time, that the teasing ceased, and their popularity grew – along with their love.

Knute was the quarterback of the high school football team and Elsa, her lisp long outgrown, was a member of the spirit squad. The couple were the obvious choice for homecoming king and queen and "Best Boy" and "Best Girl," awards.

When the two finished high school, they both worked in their families' stores, but it wasn't long before the establishments fell on hard times. The government had been subsidizing the local farmers, but stopped, allowing prices to drop back to what was natural. Because farmers had heavily invested in land when the subsidies were in place, they were now greatly in debt and couldn't make payments based on their new income. Bakery goods and chocolate were some of the first luxuries to go. Although Knute and Elsa's parents could still make a living for themselves, they couldn't include their children.

Knute's best friend – besides Elsa – was a fellow classmate named Tim. Tim had an uncle who moved to Oklahoma and was making a very good living in the oil field boom. He told Knute he was going to Oklahoma and invited the couple to come along. Knute and Elsa married in their small Lutheran church, packed their few belongings, and made the trip to the forty-sixth state.

Knute and Elsa settled about three miles northwest of a bustling town named Konawa, pronounced 'Con-uh-wa,' from the Seminole tribal language, meaning string of beads.

Konawa was located in Seminole County where the boom of 1920 was in full swing. Knute started out as an unskilled laborer – or a boll weevil, as the new hires were called. He worked long hours, only taking a few hours break to sleep. He lived in a tent city near the rigs, sometimes staying several months before going home to see his bride.

Being apart from Elsa was sometimes almost unbearable for him. Knute lived for the week long rest he would get every few months.

In the meantime, Elsa, made their little clapboard house as homey as she could. When Knute was there, she would bake all day and let him gorge himself on Krumkake, Julekake, and sour cream and raisin pies.

Elsa lived for the days Knute was home. When left alone, she not only pined for her soul mate, but also her family, and the small town Iowa life she left.

Konawa was not much larger than home, but it was different. The townspeople were very friendly and never made her feel as if she was an outsider, but still, that is how she felt.

There was no familiarity to the place. The stores were not set up on a square like in Iowa, but were instead mostly located on one main street – Broadway. Broadway wasn't called by its' name by the residents, instead it was called Main. Elsa was told it was because the Post Office was located there, along with the train depot and the most popular stores. Two of the town's four hotels, along with the restaurants which catered to them, were also located there.

The food was different too. Although most Iowans lived off their livestock and the corn, beans, and other vegetables they farmed, Elsa's family stayed true to a lot of the Norwegian ways when they could. However, it wasn't uncommon for them to dine on pork and other staples of the Iowa landscape. In Oklahoma, though, there were things she had never heard of, or seen before.

When Elsa and Knute joined the Methodist Church – because there was no Lutheran – she was often introduced to Oklahoma's exotic foods at the church suppers. She was served fried okra, a green and somewhat slimy vegetable with little seed pods that popped as you ate them. It was strange, but very tasty. There were salads made of Polk, a plant that grew wild, and was actually poisonous. It had to be boiled at least twice before it could be eaten, and Elsa never trusted that it wouldn't make her sick, so therefore she refused it each time it was offered. There was also barbeque, a spicy sauced beef or pork that had been cooked outside in a large rusty metal contraption. It ended up being one of Elsa and Knute's favorite things to eat.

However, when it came to having the staples of her Norwegian home, they were hard to come by and she often had to improvise. That too, added to her homesickness.

After about two years of marriage, Elsa noticed she had not become pregnant. She and Knute had not actually planned for a baby, but she had naturally assumed that at some point it would just happen. When she thought about it, she realized that, at first, she was so busy getting adjusted to her new life that she didn't take notice that she still received a visit from her "aunt" regularly.

One fall day however, while tooling around the house because she was bored and lonely, she reminisced back to the days of her own childhood. She remembered the love she shared with her doting mother and it was then that a yearning more fierce than anything she had ever known, surfaced.

"I want my own baby," she sighed to herself.

From that moment on, the idea was all consuming and it became her sole mission in life to become a mother.

As soon as Knute returned home, Elsa spoke to him of wanting a family. Knute was ecstatically happy with idea and the two sat in their small living room that evening, dreaming of, and making plans for, the child to come.

The soulmates' early enthusiasm waned when a year went by without Elsa becoming pregnant. Dread about even trying began to set in after the second year of being barren.

When the third year arrived, it brought their sorrow to an all-time high. Elsa and Knute quietly relinquished their dream, resigning themselves to a life without children, and settled back into the familiar landscape of just the two of them against the world.

CHAPTER TWO

During the disappointing time of not becoming parents, Knute funneled the stress he felt into his work, and in short order, made himself a standout on the rigs. In fact, before the rig foreman could give an order to fix a problem, he would find Knute already working on it.

Big and brawny, Knute could outwork the other hands two to one. Within a matter of a several weeks, he was promoted to a roustabout, and in less time than that, he became a roughneck. When he finally got time to sleep, he slept half the hours of the other hands. Sometimes the foreman would force him to stay off the rig because he would find Knute still working when he, himself had gone to bed and slept for hours.

"Knute, I admire your work ethic," he'd say, "but you're gonna get hurt if you don't get some shuteye."

Knute would reluctantly agree, but wouldn't leave until the task at hand was finished.

Day after day, Knute made himself more indispensable and became the first man entrusted to take over supervision of the rig when a foreman was called to another. There wasn't a hand, or a foreman who wavered when the rig's owner began asking about who could be trusted to have their own rig. The first name off the lips of every man who had ever worked with him, was Knute. He had been on the rigs less than nine months when he was made a foreman.

Knute's promotion came with a big raise, but it also came with a much larger time commitment. In fact, he sometimes went six months without seeing his bride. But, when Knute finally did get to go home, he threw himself into the love affair he had with Elsa. As soon as he bathed, the two made love insatiably, as if the separation had ravaged them, like acid eating through metal. It was as if their rapturous entwinement was the only way they could bring themselves to wholeness again. After, they would lay coiled and exhausted, but given new life.

It seemed their week together would be over in the blink of an eye, and Elsa would cry as Knute packed a duffle, preparing to leave her again. Each time, Elsa scolded herself, feeling selfish and ashamed, because she knew Knute was doing everything for them and their future.

Knute would take her face in his strong, calloused hands and look deep into her eyes. He would smile and tell her that it wouldn't be long until he returned, and that he would think of her every second he was away.

Because of his stoic strength, Elsa didn't know that the moment Knute was out of sight, tears would well in his eyes and his own heart would insist that it also could not bear their time apart.

After only a short time as a foreman, Knute became more than invaluable to the owner of the oil company, Daniel Stole. Daniel was a man in his sixties who had worked his way up in the fields and finally had saved enough to drill for himself. He was a good man who was trusted by all who knew him. Many of his friends were indebted to him because he allowed them to invest at the boom's startup and they were now very rich men.

Daniel instantly took a liking to Knute because he reminded him of himself – no nonsense with a "do whatever it takes to get the job done" mentality. He had also come to realize that Knute was smart. In fact, Knute had recommended some safety ideas and ways to streamline their drilling that even Daniel had not thought of in all the years he had been working the rigs. It was short order before Knute became Daniel's most trusted employee and loyal confidant.

Even though Knute knew of Daniel's fondness for him, he could have never imagined what was coming. One evening as Knute was in the southeast quadrant of the county, overseeing the Barbara Jean, Daniel drove up to the rig and told Knute to get in the truck. Knute obliged.

"Listen," Daniel said as Knute settled into the seat. "I gotta proposition for ya."

Knute raised an eyebrow.

"You are by far the best foreman I've ever had and word is getting out to other owners about you. It ain't gonna be long before they are offering you the moon and stars to come work for 'em."

Knute interrupted his boss. "I won't do that sir. You've been too good to me and I will always be loyal to you."

"I figured that's what you'd say," Daniel nodded. "But, I ain't been good enough. You have saved me thousands of dollars and probably a few lives and I owe you a lot more than you are getting paid." He looked Knute in the eye. "I want to make you my partner."

Knute sat dumbfounded for a moment, thinking he couldn't have heard the man right.

"No," he finally answered. 'You can't make me a partner just because I'm a good foreman. I don't deserve that. You've got a lot of good men working for you," Knute humbly reasoned.

"There's not a one of 'em that can touch you Knute," Daniel answered. "And I would trust you with my life. Hell I'd trust you with my family's lives. I don't have any sons and one day, I'm gonna be too old to keep this up. I already have more money than I can spend in this lifetime. It's time for me to pass it along. It's settled," he declared.

Knute tried to reject the offer again, but Daniel put his hand up to stop him from speaking.

"It's settled," he stated again and he meant it.

When he finally got home, Knute told Elsa the good news.

"We can get a bigger house Elsa. One with a huge kitchen for you to bake in," he dreamed with her.

"We will want to get another bedroom too." Elsa blushed shyly.

"Oh yes," Knute agreed. "Maybe we should get two more so our families can both stay longer at Christmas."

"Maybe we should get a four bedroom then." Elsa slyly smiled.

"That might be a little too big," Knute scratched his head. "We don't want to go overboard."

"Well if we have a room for each of our parents, a room for ourselves and then one for the baby, it's going to take four."

Knute started to sigh, thinking that Elsa still had not given up on the dream of having a baby. Just as he had begun to reestablish that they would be fine without a child, he saw her smile, followed by the glow on her face, and finally the somewhat small bump in her stomach. It was hard for him to believe he hadn't noticed it before.

"Elsa," he gasped. "Are you with child?"

The world seemed to stop spinning, as his own words sunk in – with child.

"We are having a baby, Knute. We are having a baby!" Elsa laughed.

Knute picked her up and twirled her around. He whooped and hollered like a banshee. Then he actually did a little jig.

"I can't believe it! After all this time!" he beamed.

The timing couldn't have been better. Since Knute had become a partner, he no longer had to be on the rig sites overnight and even though he still put in long hours, coming home exhausted most nights, at least he was home. Knute didn't let Elsa out of his sight.

For Knute, it was as if Elsa was the first woman to have ever become pregnant. He treated her as if she were a fragile egg.

"Knute, stop fussing over me so much," Elsa teased. "I'm just fine. In fact, I've never been better." She would put her hands on her hips for extra emphasis. Knute, however, ignored her, doting on her every chance he got. He would even offer to fix their dinner.

"Knute you can do many things, but cooking isn't one of them," she teased.

Elsa couldn't help but smile when after supper, she would watch Knute as he napped in his favorite chair. Life was as good as it could possibly be.

The baby was born in March and Knute and Elsa brought her home to a two-story, four bedroom Victorian house they purchased a few months earlier. It was located just a mile east of their old place and sat on 80 acres of pasture land with areas of wooded groves tucked into the landscape. They named her Trudy Mariah.

CHAPTER THREE

Trudy grew up the center of her parents' lives. She especially had Knute wrapped tighter than a rubber band, around her little finger.

"Come on Daddy!" the child would squeal when they played. "Chase me!"

Knute would raise his arms like a monster and stumble after her, half way growling and laughing. Trudy would scream even louder and make a bee line to hide behind her mother's skirt.

"Help me Mamma!" she cried. "It's a big scawey monster!"

"No monsters are going to get my baby today!" Elsa would place her hands on her hips and pretend to crossly glare at Knute. "Should we shoo him with a broom?" she asked her little blue-eyed beauty.

"Uh HUH!" Trudy would yell, to which Knute would immediately surrender.

"No brooms," he would laugh. "Monsters are very afraid of brooms!"

Trudy would emerge from behind her mother and run giggling into her father's arms.

"I wuv you Daddy," she smiled as she kissed his cheek.

Knute would always tear up a tiny bit hearing those precious words.

Trudy was just as smart, if not smarter, than her parents had been at her age. Like her mother, she was reading long before she entered school. She could also write the alphabet, her first and last name and several things she saw around their homestead.

Chicken was her favorite word to write because of the K. When her mother taught her the letters, she told Trudy to remember the K as a cheerleader.

"See, it puts its arm up here and its leg down here," she explained, showing the tiny girl how to draw the lines. "I used to do that for Daddy when he played football," she reminisced.

After they did their lessons, the two would go outside and pretend to cheer for their "team," which consisted of their milk cow, Ursula, and the plow horses, Buttercup and Rufus.

"Go Buttercup! Go Rufus! Go, go, Buttercup and Rufus!" they chanted.

Trudy's favorite cheer was the firecracker cheer.

"Fiew Cwacker, fiew cwacker, boom, boom, boom," she'd chant. "Da boys got da muscle, da teachews got da bwains, da girwls got da pwetty wegs and we win da game!" Trudy would jump in the air and kick her bottom with her heels before she and her mother would roll to the ground laughing.

The days spent with her mother and father, playing, exploring the land, catching fireflies and fishing for crawdads were nothing short of perfect. Trudy could not remember a time when she had been happier.

When she finally got old enough to attend school though, things drastically changed and Trudy was ostracized from day one.

On her first day, she was very excited. She had spent all her life with grownups and although she had seen other children at church and in town, she had never been with them, not even to play. She anticipated that before the day was over, she would have a playmate – maybe more than one.

The teacher introduced herself to the small class. Trudy was very attentive. As Mrs. Martin turned to draw an apple on the chalkboard, Trudy felt someone yank one of the blond curly locks on her head. She squealed and the class erupted in laughter. Mrs. Martin swung around to see Trudy standing beside her desk, holding the back of her head.

"Trudy!" the teacher scolded. "We don't yell out in class. What is wrong with you?"

Robert, the boy who had done the yanking, sat quietly hiding his guilt. Trudy looked back at the boy, waiting for him to confess what he had done, but instead he mouthed to her, "I'll get ya," and Trudy took the warning to heart.

"I'm sorwy," she told her teacher and again the classroom erupted.

"I'm sorwy," a little dirty faced girl taunted.

"Enough of this nonsense!" their teacher warned and the class became quiet again.

Trudy didn't understand why the other children were being mean to her. She wanted more than anything to be accepted and she went out of her way to be friendly, although she was extremely shy. But, as the days went by, things became worse for her. She was unaware that she had a perfect trifecta of reasons to be disliked.

First of all, Trudy had very nice clothes – much nicer than most of the children. Second, she was very smart and her teacher continuously made it known how impressed she was with Trudy's intelligence. Third, she was beautiful and other little girls who wore hand me downs and sometimes didn't even have shoes that fit, were jealous with a capital J.

When day after day, not one child was willing to befriend her, Trudy began to hate school. After months of verbal and sometimes physical abuse, she learned to abhor it, especially since it seemed as if her assailants tried to make a game of who could humiliate her the most.

The taunting went from Robert pulling her hair that first day, to putting gum in it weeks later. Then, a boy named Jeffery took his scissors and actually cut off a large section of Trudy's hair, leaving what was left to fan out like a plucked chicken.

The little girl who had taunted her over the way she pronounced sorry, mercilessly mocked Trudy every time she opened her mouth. She told her to stop talking like a baby and asked her if she still wore diapers. All the other kids laughed and several tried to look under her dress to see if she did.

A girl named Penny would find Trudy at recess and take her shoes, filling them with dirt. Even the smallest child in the glass, Henry, often took a stick and poked her, telling her to gallop like a horse. When Trudy refused, he would strike her with it.

Trudy's parents paid a visit to the school after the haircutting incident and they were assured that a close eye would be kept on their daughter. The next day, when the class was made to write "I will not bully," one hundred times, Trudy was ambushed. As all the girls were sent to the bathroom to wash their hands to the bathroom before lunch, they cornered her.

"You're a tattletale!" they hissed. "If you ever tattle again, you'll be sorry!" They warned her.

Trudy was terrified. After all they had already done to her, she couldn't even imagine what unspeakable punishment they might have in store for her. When she got off the bus, and her mother asked her if she had been bullied that day, Trudy wanted more than anything to tell her that she had. However, the idea that she could be subjected to even worse things than she had already endured, forced her to remain silent. She flatly denied it and Elsa, none the wiser, smiled.

"That's wonderful news Trudy!" She kissed her daughter on the forehead. "I'm so glad we have this all straightened out."

Although Trudy's teacher did try to keep an eye on her, the offenders managed to keep their actions covert. They saved their torment for times when Trudy was isolated, like on the playground or in the bathroom. They also managed to sabotage her desk with insects and rodents before and after school.

Her parents struggled daily to get her onto the school bus, however, they failed to realize the real reason for their child's reluctance.

"Knute, Trudy's teacher, sent a note home that Trudy won't sit still," Elsa reported one evening.

They could have never dreamed that it was because Robert had put ants in her desk.

"Mrs. Martin sent another note with Trudy saying she yells out in class," Elsa announced.

Neither she nor Knute understood it was because Jeffery was sticking her with pins.

"Mrs. Martin says that Trudy is sullen and won't answer questions when asked." Elsa shook her head, dumbfounded because at home, Trudy was a chatter box.

Of course they didn't know that the sweet, loving and talkative child they knew, was terrified of being accused of being a baby wearing diapers because of her speech impediment.

Every note they received from school made the Dahl's more perplexed but it still didn't dawn on them that their only child was being unmercifully tormented. In fact, they finally decided that Trudy just didn't like being away from them and they told themselves, she would outgrow it.

Although each day when the bus arrived, Trudy would bellow, begging her mother not to make her go, she was forced to get on the bus.

CHAPTER FOUR

S ummers were what Trudy lived for. Every year her grandparents would visit for at least a month and they spoiled her almost as much as her parents did. She and Knute's father would take walks down to Jumper Creek and catch tadpoles and turtles. Knute's mother taught her the art of chocolate making.

Elsa's father, pretended to be her very own horse and let her ride his back across their parlor floor. Elsa's mother shared the family secret to making Kringla. Trudy wished the days of summer would never end, but invariably they did and with the worst of dread, she and her mother would begin preparations for the coming school year.

Trudy's greatest tormenter was a girl named Loretta Lankford. Loretta herself was for the most part a loner, although she did manage from time to time to bring a coven of hateful girls on board to condemn each and every thing Trudy did, said, or wore.

Trudy spent hours trying to remember what it was she had done to offend the girl who had taken a dislike to her from the first day of school. She replayed every second of every interaction she had with the girl, but there was nothing she could remember. In fact, the first interaction was one in which Trudy, had tried to make Loretta her friend. On that day when Mrs. Martin told her to take a seat, Trudy had looked at the girl to her left and smiled sweetly at her.

"Hi," Trudy shyly said.

Loretta scoffed while looking her over from head to toe. Trudy, had blushed, not knowing because of the girl's reaction, if she looked funny, or something worse. From that point forward, the only words from Loretta's mouth were vindictive, sarcastic and mean. As the years passed, the bullying intensified.

"Your nose is hideous," Loretta spat. "Your eyes look like blue bird poop," she hissed. "You bleach your hair 'cause the real color is green like a Martian. You have disgusting knees. You have big feet. You should do us all a favor and drop dead."

The insults were never ending.

With each beginning school year, knowing what awaited her, and wanting terribly to make it stop, Trudy's resolve to solve the puzzle increased. In the beginning the potential answers were benign enough. *"Maybe she thought I sneered at her on that first day,"* Trudy reasoned. *"Maybe I remind her of someone who hurt her."*

But as the years passed, Trudy, still unable to find an appropriate answer, began to believe the insults spewed by her tormentor. *"Maybe I am ugly and my parents just tell me I'm pretty so they don't hurt my feelings,"* she decided. *"Maybe they buy me nice clothes to try to make up for my ugly face."*

The more insults that were hurled, the darker her own self-loathing became.

"I'm disgusting," she would tell herself when looking in the mirror to brush her teeth."

When her mother took her shopping, she refused to buy bright colors, insisting on dull beiges, grays and blacks. She also refused to buy a size eight shoe, and forced her foot into a size seven and a half. She spent hours in the mirror looking at her nose, putting her finger down the bridge to see how it would look if most of it were gone. She stopped looking others in the eye for fear they would find her blue eyes morbid. There was nothing on Trudy's body that she liked. In fact, she loathed it all and if she could have, she would have ceased to exist.

Trudy got used to being alone. She buried herself in her work and in reading. She never got anything below an A in any subject. Even though she didn't care for history, she made sure she was attentive and focused. Although Mr. Lowden often asked questions of his class, Trudy never dared raise her hand. She knew the answers, but she wasn't about to bring attention to herself. Being in school was very much her prison. Her heart wanted to participate in and out of the classroom, but the fear of being criticized never left her and she could not find the courage to step outside herself and be who she really thought she should be – until she was twelve.

That fateful summer, Trudy's parents took her on a day trip into Maiden. Maiden was much bigger than Konawa and there were boutiques, quaint restaurants, and an elaborate and beautifully decorated movie theater named The Majesty.

After a day of shopping and eating, Trudy and her parents walked into the enormous lobby adorned with gold ropes, burgundy velvet drapes, and matching burgundy carpeting.

There were two grand staircases on either side, both with mahogany and golden banisters. It was the most luxurious place she had ever seen. She thought it could have been a palace.

The trio ordered popcorn and sodas before they were shown to their seats. The young man escorting them wore a uniform which resembled that of the Nutcrackers that Trudy's mother put out at Christmas time. Trudy sat back, engrossed in the auditorium, with its large stage, until the lights dimmed and a magnificent, two story high curtain rose to reveal an equally large white screen. Trudy was mesmerized.

The movie was entitled *Little Lord Fauntleroy* and starred Freddie Bartholomew. Trudy was in awe of the young actor, who couldn't have been older than she was. Seeing him on the big screen, acting out a heart wrenching story, was the closest thing she had ever experienced to a miracle. It was as if Jesus himself had come down and anointed her with the truth. This was what she was to do with her life. Being an actress, she knew from the deepest depths of her soul, was her life's calling.

When they left the theatre, Trudy's head was swimming. She sat in silence on most of the ride home, consumed with figuring out how to make her dream come true. Being an actress, she believed, could transport her from the life she had been forced to live, to one she could only dream of. Every role would allow her the escape she had spent years longing for. Being an actress would be the answer to all her prayers. She could leave her prison behind forever, never again having to be Trudy.

"Mother," she finally said, "I want to be an actress."

Her mother, not really understanding her daughter's fantasy, told her they would visit the theater again, when a suitable picture was showing.

"No!" she put her head up against the front seat of their 1933 Chevy Eagle. "I don't want to see another movie, I want to be an actress!" she exclaimed.

Elsa laughed. "Oh Sweetie," she placated, "that's impossible. Actors and actresses live in California and New York. We live in Oklahoma."

"Soooo?" Trudy whined. "That doesn't matter, you can take me there. Please Mommy, please!"

Her mother shook her head and turned to look at her blue eyed princess. "Honey, you are certainly beautiful enough to be an actress, but there is no way we can go to California or New York. What would your father do without us?"

What Elsa and Knute thought was a passing fancy, turned out to be anything but. Trudy was relentless. Every morning the first thing she would say upon wakening was "Can we go to California or New York?" which was followed by begging and pleading until Elsa or Knute forbid her from asking again. The last question at night was the same, and again, it was followed by begging that usually ended in tearful sobbing when the answer remained "No."

"What are we going to do about this?" Elsa asked Knute when they finally climbed into bed, after an overly trying night. "How are we going to get this idea of California and New York out of the child's head?"

Knute lay staring at their bedroom ceiling for several moments.

"Let's bring it to her," he finally answered.

Elsa sat up and looked at him.

"Let's let her put on plays and act here," he explained. "I'll build her a stage. We can even build a bench to sit and watch her," he surmised.

"Oh yes!" Elsa answered. "Yes Knute that is exactly what we should do! You are a genius my dear husband – a genius!"

The following day, Knute got to work on a stage which he constructed right behind their house. By the late afternoon, he had completed the base and the floor.

"What are you doing Daddy?" Trudy asked him when she rounded the house and almost ran into the platform.

"We can't go to California or New York," he answered her, "but that doesn't mean that you can't be an actress. This is yours and by this time tomorrow," he told his child, "you will have a completed stage upon which to work."

Trudy's mouth hit the ground. "Really?!" she squealed with delight. "Really Daddy?!"

"Absolutely," he answered, "So you better get to work on your first performance."

Trudy ran into the house, yelling for her mother.

"You must take me to the library," she ordered. "I have to get a play. I have a performance to give!"

Elsa was more than happy to oblige the girl. Especially if it meant that the whining and tantrums were coming to an end.

CHAPTER FIVE

Trudy's first play was *Craig's Wife*. She played Harriet
Craig, a woman who was obsessed with keeping her house
clean. There were several parts where Trudy didn't need
another actor, but on the parts she did, she just explained to her
parents what was happening and she developed the dialogue to
be one sided. Her parents praised her abilities and this fueled
the all-consuming fire, even more.

From the moment Trudy set foot on her new stage she felt
as if she were home. The plays were a refuge from her
tormented and bullied life as a school girl. Memorizing her lines
completely replaced the taunts that usually replayed themselves
in her head. Rehearsing the dialogue until it was second nature,
left no room for her to dwell on the harsh ridicule she was
subjected to daily. The plays and her acting gave her the escape
she needed to survive and it was a good thing because
unfortunately, as Trudy grew, so did the taunting. Each day her
beauty became more apparent, especially when she hit puberty.

Although the boys had once taunted her, they were now drooling over her, and that made the girls loathe her even more.

"Look at her," Eleanor Marcum, hissed one day in gym class. "I bet she stuffs her bra. Don't you Trudy?" she yelled across the locker room. The rest of the girls howled.

"You think you're soooo special," Janice Halbert declared. "Just because you have nice clothes and your daddy has money, you think you're better than us. Well you ain't! You ain't nothin' but a snot-nosed, spoiled rotten, brat."

Trudy shook her head, wanting the taunters to understand that she didn't think she was better than them. However, it went unnoticed and they continued their assaults.

"You smell funny too," Edith Mosely held her nose. "Why do you always smell like that?" she sneered.

The locker room erupted. Trudy didn't understand why they thought she smelled. She always bathed, and with lavender soap.

"I bet she takes baths in a golden tub filled with milk," Edith shamed.

"She may take milk baths," Bea Warner said, "but it's sour!" She laughed out loud, and the rest of the girls followed suit.

Bea continued her insults. "You may take a bath in a fancy tub, but it still won't take the stink off ya," she spat.

Trudy felt tears begin to sting her eyes. She didn't have a golden tub. She didn't take milk baths. Why were the girls making those things up? The tears tried making their escape, but Trudy wasn't about to give her bullies the satisfaction. She turned to face her locker and took a deep breath, trying to calm herself.

"Just ignore them; just ignore them," she told herself.

Every day she was at school, the badgering continued. One day they would insult her shoes. "Did your rich daddy hire elves from France?" they mocked.

Another day, they made fun of her hair. "You go to New York to get that dye job?" one of them asked.

"More like the Piggly Wiggly," another cackled. "After all it looks like a bunch of curly pig's tails!"

The worst blow came from none other than Loretta Lankford. Trudy had turned thirteen just a few weeks earlier and had fully blossomed into a young woman.

"I heard you've been having fun with the entire football team. You're loose." she declared. "You're nothing more than a harlot."

It took no coaxing from Loretta for the rest of the girls to jump on the bandwagon. It happened so quickly, Trudy didn't know what hit her.

"Yeah, I heard you even do thaaaat," Anita Bellow, opened her mouth into an O.

"On every single one of them," Josephine Walters, scoffed.

"She's disgusting," Madeline Mullins said.

"Yeah," a chorus of other girls agreed.

Trudy felt her face go hot and her legs begin to buckle. She sat down on the bench beside the lockers and turned her back to her accusers. She wanted to run from there as fast as she could, but her body wouldn't cooperate. Her head swam in the sewage they had unleashed on her. Surely they didn't really believe the lies they were creating. Surely they knew she was pure. She prayed that they were just being mean and would forget the entire thing as soon as they left the locker room.

But, they didn't.

The following day as she walked down the hall to her Algebra class, every single head turned to watch her. The girls backed up to their lockers as if they would catch fire if she got near them. The boys, leered – some licking their lips while obviously lusting after her. Whispers surfaced and by the time she reached her class, they had reached a crescendo of every kind of lie that could be told about her.

Trudy was sick to her stomach. She tried to sit in her chair and pay attention to her teacher, but the whispers kept invading her head.

"The whole team," she heard from two girls.

"I got her," a boy had boasted.

"Yeah, so did I," another countered.

"She's a tramp," she heard from a circle of the Spirit Girls.

"May I be excused," Trudy asked her teacher. "I'm not feeling well."

"Of course dear," Mrs. Smith told her. "You don't look well Trudy. Maybe you should go home."

Trudy did, and there she stayed for the rest of the week.

"You don't have a fever Honey," her mother had said. "But you are very pale. Maybe we should go see Dr. Brandon?"

Trudy told her mother she didn't need to see the doctor, that she would be better in a couple of days.

"I just need some rest, Mother," she brooded. "I promise I'll get better."

Elsa catered to her daughter, bringing her soup and crackers, even some ice cream. Trudy stayed in bed, wrapped in covers, while writing frantically. Her mother assumed she was working on the homework she was missing and didn't pay any mind to it.

Finally, late Friday afternoon, Trudy decided to take a bath and dress. On Saturday, she returned to her stage and began preparation for her newest creation, one that she had written herself.

Trudy rehearsed her play most of the day while waiting for her father to return from checking on a new rig, and her mother to complete errands she had in town. When both parents were home and settled, she asked them to come and watch her newest creation.

As soon as Elsa and Knute were seated, Trudy wrapped herself up in a ball and did summersaults across the stage, stopping in the center. There she began to unwrap, stretching her arms above her head, raising her torso from the floor, and finally standing fully upright. She looked up at the sky and then let a blood curdling and primal scream escape her lips.

Her mother jumped, taken aback at her daughter's outburst.

Knute looked at his wife, the strangeness of the moment revealing itself on his face.

"I once was beautiful!" Trudy yelled. "But no more," she barely whispered. "What was divine, now wretched," she preached.

"What was born to sunlight, now enslaved to the darkness. The ghouls and gremlins of the night are my only friends," she narrowed her eyes, and hissed.

Elsa took a deep breath, trying to calm herself and not let Trudy see that what she was saying and doing were more than disturbing.

"And you!" she pointed right at both her parents, "You perpetuated the fantasy," she cackled. "But I see the truth now. There will be no more hiding it."

Trudy circled herself wringing her hands then swatting at her hair.

"It can never be hidden again," she sighed. "Even love can't keep it a secret," she sing-songed. "What you thought was real," she turned to her parents again. "was only an illusion – a mere shadow made to look larger and more looming by the blinding sun." Trudy threw her hands up, pointing to the orange ball in the sky.

She circled herself again, finally stopping to plant both feet at edge of the front of the stage. "The blinding sun has revealed the truth," she restated, "and all must end!" Trudy fell forward off the stage and into her parents, Knute jumping up to break her fall.

Trudy stood up and then bowed as if she were receiving a standing ovation to a packed house at the Lyceum Theater in New York City.

Her mother and father looked at each other, mouths open, wondering what had just happened. Elsa, finally got herself together and was the first to clap, although hesitantly. When

Knute eventually recovered his senses, he followed his wife's lead.

"That was splendid my dear," Elsa choked, and brushed non-existent wrinkles from her dress. She looked at Knute again, smiling this time, trying to pretend that everything was normal.

"Um, yes, darling, that was wonderful," her father agreed.

In the meantime, Trudy returned to her stage and continued to bow, looking all around as if she were truly seeing an adoring audience. She waved, smiled and blew kisses to those who weren't really there.

"Oh my goodness," her mother swallowed. "It's time to get dinner started. Come on dear," she said to Trudy. "Come help Mommy make dinner, okay?"

Trudy continued waving and blowing kisses.

"Honey?" Elsa walked to the stage directly in front of Trudy. "Come help Mommy make dinner." She tugged at Trudy's skirt. Trudy snapped back to reality.

"What?" she said, startled. "What Mother?"

"I need you to help me with dinner," her mother replied, turning to see if Knute realized that Trudy had really taken a leave of absence. Knute was ashen, but covered his confusion.

"Well, we better get going," he told them. "It's going to be dark soon."

Trudy walked to the side of the stage and bounded down the stairs. She entered the back door of the house, smiling as if her "performance" was the most natural thing in the world.

CHAPTER SIX

The following Monday, Trudy returned to school, but with a new found confidence. The girls in the locker room continued to taunt her, but it was as if she couldn't hear them. She whistled to herself as she dressed for gym class and, she actually skipped a little out of the room. The girls looked at each other wondering what had changed.

They weren't about to let it go though. Trudy had for too long, been an easy mark. Each day they continued to taunt and tease, but still Trudy ignored them. It was as if she was somewhere else and they didn't even exist. The satisfaction that had long been a payoff of their actions wasn't nearly as satisfactory as before.

Even Loretta Lankford tried upping her game, much to her own dismay. A week later, she cornered Trudy in the restroom. While Trudy was turned, washing her hands, Loretta threw ketchup on her pants, making it appear as if Trudy was on her period and blood had seeped through her clothing. Trudy, simply turned to Loretta and said, "Hmm, would you look at that?" before taking a towel and cleaning herself up. She then tied her sweater around her small waist and hummed *Dream a Little Dream of Me*, as she walked out the door. What Loretta had thought was going to be the Pièce de résistance of all her bullying, was nothing more than a complete dud.

Still, Loretta wasn't going to give up. Two days later, she again cornered Trudy in the restroom. This time she brought with her Anita Bellow and Madeline Mullins.

"Get her," Loretta ordered the two, who each grabbed one of Trudy's arms.

"Put her where she belongs," Loretta spat, pointing to the large metal trash can in the corner.

The two girls, who thought they would have to forcefully shove Trudy toward the corner, were surprised when Trudy voluntarily walked. The ease in which Trudy moved, in contrast to the force the girls had put forward, caused them both to lunge forward and fall. Trudy simply bent over to help the tormentors up. She even brushed them off.

After the two realized that they had fallen instead of Trudy, embarrassed, they ran out of the room. Loretta, seeing her plan had failed, left too.

It only took a few more instances of Trudy being oblivious to Loretta's attempts at humiliating her, for the girl to stop trying. It was a frustration that the bully had never known before, and even when she would dream up some wicked scheme against Trudy, her belief that it could backfire turned the tables. The enjoyment was finally gone.

After that, Trudy's life continued to improve. Her teachers adored her. She was the perfect student in every way. If they gave an assignment, they could bet everything they owned that Trudy would not only do it, but do it better than anyone else in the class. When it came time for the spring scholastic competitions, the teachers fought over which subjects she would represent.

Trudy's parents couldn't contain their pride. When she would return home with yet another scholastic medal, they would lavish her with gifts, chocolates or her favorite dinner. They would talk for days about her achievements, and praise her as if she were Einstein himself. Trudy loved the attention.

The adulation, which was now becoming much more mainstream than the taunts, allowed for Trudy's self-esteem to begin growing again. By the time she finished junior high, she had convinced herself that she might just in fact, be as wonderful as her parents and teachers thought.

Best of all, the success to which she had become accustomed allowed her to leave behind the memories of the dark and anguishing bullying, as if they had never occurred.

When Trudy got into high school, her dreams came true. As she looked over the class offerings, she could not believe what she saw. There was a class for speech and drama. Trudy felt as if she had died and gone to heaven, especially when her teacher announced that they were going to be performing three plays during the year.

The first play they performed was *The Glass Menagerie*, by Tennessee Williams. Although Trudy had never performed the play on her own stage, the moment she read the script, she knew she was meant to play the part of Laura. The play was based on the life of Williams, who was really named Thomas.

In the play, Laura was the older sister of the main character, Tom. Due to circumstances which made her somewhat of an outsider, Laura isolated herself, and made her own world. Trudy felt as if she and Laura were kindred spirits. She knew there was no one who could play the part better and Trudy was right. The play and her performance were all the town talked about for weeks.

Trudy, of course, threw everything she had into her drama class. After the first two plays, Miss Danton, the drama instructor, began picking plays with Trudy in mind. The final play of Trudy's freshman year was *Dream Girl*.

Many girls tried out for the lead, but it wasn't even close. Trudy was given the part of Georgina Allerton, a flighty, day-dreaming bookstore manager, and again, it made Trudy the talk of the town.

Jealousy, especially among those that didn't get the parts they wanted, continued to rear its ugly head, but Trudy was immune to it. The life she lived on the stage was what she thought of as her real life. Each character became a part of who she was. With every new one, the shy, tortured girl grew weaker, and the self-confident artist, grew stronger. By the end of her sophomore year, when she not only participated in the plays at school, but in Community Theater in Maiden, the girl known as Trudy Dahl was only a shadow of her former self.

CHAPTER SEVEN

T rudy continued to grow in her beauty and the boys fell at her feet. She never noticed them though. Many of them, she knew, had defiled her name in the past, and she wasn't about to give them reason to continue. Her mother and father fielded calls on a daily basis from local boys asking to speak to their daughter. Her parents revealed the caller's identification only to have Trudy shake her head no, forcing them to take a message. Those messages were quickly disposed of by Trudy, who never even bothered to read them.

Trudy's dismissals became legendary. Every boy in school wanted to be "the one" who finally managed to get Trudy to go out with him. They showered her with stuffed animals, lockets, chocolates, and flowers, only to have them returned. Young men followed her down the halls, ready to fall at her feet and worship her. She acted as if she couldn't even see them. They congregated at her locker, trying to engage her in small talk, before she would politely nod and walk away. Not one of them had even managed to get Trudy to acknowledge his existence. That was until she met Paul Somerton at the end of her sophomore year.

On the final night of Trudy's drama class performance of *Victoria Regina,* a strapping young man, tall, blond, and exceptionally handsome, attended the after party with his aunt, Trudy's drama teacher.

Trudy sat on an overstuffed club chair in the corner of Miss Danton's living room, watching the other cast members laugh, make small talk and drink punch. She didn't want to be there, but as the star of the play, she was obligated.

She twiddled her thumbs and sighed, then straightened her skirt. She looked at her shoes, noticing a small scuff on the left one. She looked around the room again before fingering a small porcelain figurine of a dog, which sat on the accent table beside her. She was lost in her own thoughts, wishing the minutes away so that she could leave, when she was startled by a light tap on her shoulder.

"You were really good tonight," the most handsome boy she had ever seen, said to her. "I'm Paul Somerton." The young man stuck out his hand to shake Trudy's.

Trudy stopped breathing. She had never seen a boy more beautiful. It was as if she were meeting her very first male movie star. Actually, he was better than a movie star – even better looking than Laurence Olivier. The boy had eyes almost as blue as Trudy's. His blond hair was more ash colored in comparison to Trudy's golden blond. He was muscular with a strong and confident jaw.

Trudy swallowed hard, unsure of how to react.

"Umm, thank you," she finally managed.

"My aunt has been telling me what a great actress you are," he stated.

"Your aunt?" Trudy questioned.

"Oh, yes. Sorry. Miss Danton's my aunt. She wanted me to come see the play tonight. She said it would be a great history lesson, so I did," he smiled. "Like I said, you were killer-diller."

Trudy blushed, folded her hands on her lap and then smiled. She was at a total loss for words.

"Do you mind if I sit here," Paul asked, pointing toward a green sofa next to Trudy's chair.

Trudy nodded her approval.

"I go to Ashton," he said. "I'm a sophomore. What about you?"

"I'm a sophomore too," she shyly smiled.

"What else do you like to do besides plays?" Paul leaned into her.

"I like school," she replied.

"Oh no," she thought to herself, *"That was such a stupid answer. He's going to think I'm such a fathead."* She began to panic before Paul eased her suffering.

"I really do too." He smiled showing deep and endearing dimples. "I know we aren't supposed to, but I like learning about new things and other places, especially since we live in such small towns." He laughed.

Trudy laughed along with him. She was extremely happy that Paul didn't think her answer was dumb.

The two continued their conversation, never even noticing that everyone had left the party except them. Finally, Paul's aunt interrupted them.

"Trudy, I see you've met Paul. How lovely. I'm afraid though that I have to get him back home and seeing that it is so late, we've got to get going. Would you like me to drop you off at home? You live right on the way."

Trudy didn't hesitate because it meant she could spend more time with Paul.

"That would be nice," she smiled at her teacher and then phoned her parents to inform them.

Trudy learned on the ride home that Paul was the pitcher for Ashton's High School's baseball team. Trudy was impressed because Ashton continuously had one of the best teams in the state, having won state championships seven out of the past ten years.

The best thing she learned during the ride however was that Paul was interested in her.

"You should come to our next game." He invited. "It's Tuesday after school."

"I'd like that," Trudy eagerly answered. "I'll have to ask my mother if she can take me though."

"I would be happy to take you Trudy," Miss Danton interrupted, trying to hide her surprise. "I go to most of Paul's games."

Trudy told her teacher she would ask permission from her parents and let her know. They pulled up the long driveway to Trudy's house before Paul got the courage to ask if he could phone her. Trudy thought she would faint.

"Of course," she smiled sweetly, as she slipped a small piece of paper and pencil from her bag and wrote the number down.

"I'll see you next week then?" Paul's own smile lit up the night.

"I hope so," Trudy replied, before turning to skip to her porch.

Trudy rushed into her house, dropping her purse on the stairs, before running into the kitchen where her mother and father sat having coffee at a small wooden farm table.

"You're home later than usual," her mother remarked. "Did you have a good…"

Before Elsa could finish her sentence, Trudy interrupted. "Mother, may I go to Ashton with Miss Danton on Tuesday? I've been invited to watch her nephew pitch at their baseball game." Trudy bubbled with excitement.

Both Elsa and Knute looked at each other, stunned. Although boys had been calling for almost two years, they had gotten used to idea that Trudy was never going to date. In fact, it had been a topic of many late night conversations between the two.

"Do you think we should make her date?" Elsa had asked Knute. "She needs to be a teenager. She needs to have friends." Her mother fretted.

"She'll date when she's ready I guess. Maybe she just wants to concentrate on her school work and her plays," Knute reasoned. "We really shouldn't treat this like it's a problem," he told his wife. "We are lucky that she is so smart and studious."

"I know," Elsa agreed, "but I don't think it's normal. It worries me how she won't even give a boy a chance. What if she ends up alone for her whole life? What if she never learns to have a relationship other than what she has with her family?"

During that time, Knute would try to soothe Elsa's concerns, telling her that eventually Trudy would find someone who interested her.

It appeared she finally had.

"Hmm," Elsa cleared her throat, trying not to give away her complete elation. "Well, Father, what do you think?"

Knute also feigned concern as he bit his lower lip as if in thought.

"Oh, I don't know Trudy. Who is this boy? Is he someone we know?"

"Like I said," Trudy excitedly explained, "he's Miss Danton's nephew. His name is Paul, Paul Somerton. He's a sophomore, just like me. He's really good in school. He even likes school, just like me."

Trudy began making her case. "He's the pitcher for Ashton. You know they won state last year. He was the pitcher then!" she boasted to her father. "Dad, you have probably seen him play considering how much you like baseball. You probably saw him play against us. Please, please Dad, let me go," she begged.

Knute could no longer watch his daughter suffer. He sighed as if it were really causing him pain to give her permission.

"Oh alright, if it means that much to you. But, only if you have your school work done and, what about drama class? Don't you all practice after school?"

"Not anymore," Trudy jumped up and down. "We're done now that we've put on the last play of the year."

She wrapped her arms around her father, followed by her mother. Then she squealed while running up the stairs to her room.

Trudy never thought there would come a day when she would be glad she did not have play rehearsals. But things had changed. Things had indeed changed.

CHAPTER EIGHT

Trudy could not think of anything other than the boy she had met hours earlier. She lay on her bed quietly saying his name.

"Paul," she sighed breathlessly.

Why did she feel this way? She understood that she didn't know who he really was, but from the moment she laid eyes on him, she felt as if she were finally home. Although her childhood years at home with her parents had been wonderful, she had never been able to put her finger on why she felt different until that moment. But it finally all made sense.

Trudy had grown up watching the two people who raised her, as a duo. She was the third wheel of the group. Even though she knew her parents loved her fiercely, she surmised that she could never be a part of what they shared together. Her father, adored – no, he worshiped her mother. Her mother, she feared, would not continue to breathe if something ever happened to her father.

Feeling the new connection to Paul, she was able to understand that the relationship her parents had was meant only for them and what did that make her? The two had a bond that was impenetrable – even by their own daughter. She realized that the tiny bit of uncomfortableness that she had lived with was because she had always been an outsider.

Trudy was a little distraught with the realization that, although she was a part of their relationship and she was a result of the relationship, she could, and never would, be inside the relationship. Knute and Elsa were one before she was born; they would be one when she left to attend college. She would always be standing outside the window looking in.

On the other hand, Trudy was also a little mesmerized with the idea that she too could have a relationship like her parents. The boys at school were so, well, sophomoric. They weren't capable of understanding the depths of true love. They didn't have a clue about its meaning. Truthfully, until that moment, neither had she. Finding Paul – discovering a feeling she had never before known – had opened her eyes, revealing the truth. Trudy had only been half herself for the first sixteen years of her life.

Trudy finally tore herself away from her contemplation long enough to dress for bed and brush her teeth. She crawled under the covers and waited for sleep to come. It didn't. Instead her thoughts raced from her first words to Paul to the last glance she had of him as she left the car. She replayed every single second of their evening together and she excitedly anticipated his call and their next meeting, not knowing if she could wait until Tuesday to see him again.

Trudy awoke, sleepily rolling over to stare at the ceiling. Had the previous night been a dream? Did it really happen? Did the person named Paul Somerton truly exist? Trudy heard her parents moving around the kitchen, her mother fixing their breakfast before they would leave to attend church services.

"Trudy? Honey, it's time to get up. We have church in an hour," she heard her mother call from below.

Trudy didn't want to go. She just wanted to remain in her bed and revisit the previous night's events. But, how could she explain that to her parents? She reluctantly washed her face, and brushed her teeth and hair. She dabbed a little lipstick and rouge on her pale face before walking to her window to look over the dawning of the day.

Being March, it was still cold in Oklahoma. Sometimes, winter liked to show everyone who was boss by unexpectedly dumping several inches of snow on the ground. Today had been one of those days. Trudy prowled through her closet finally settling on her ivory cashmere sweater set and an ankle length rose colored skirt. She dreamily put on her shoes while her mind was consumed with the answer to a prayer she hadn't even known she prayed – the answer of the love of her life, Paul Somerton.

Sunday came and went. Trudy had tried to study for a history test she was to have on Tuesday, but couldn't concentrate. She gave up before putting on galoshes, and traipsing through the snow into the wooded grove behind her family's home.

She walked through the trees, truly seeing for the first time in her life, their stunning beauty.

"Why haven't I ever noticed this before?" she wondered.

A flash of red above caught her eye. A red-bellied woodpecker perched high in a dead oak, watching her. She had never remembered the feathered tuffs of its head being so red. It was as if it was lit from the inside out. The bird was nothing short of breath-taking.

Trudy found a fallen log near Jumper Creek, tucked her woolen coat beneath her, and sat down.

"Paul," she sighed. "I wonder what he is doing right now?" she asked herself before coming to the realization that if he actually phoned her today, she wasn't close enough to the house to hear her mother's announcement.

Trudy jumped from her seat and ran as quickly as she could back to the house. She tore up the back porch and through the door, into the kitchen where her mother was peeling potatoes.

"Mother, has anyone called?" she breathlessly inquired.

"Why no, Sweetheart," came the most undesirable of replies.

Trudy's heart sank. She stood, galoshes dripping, for several minutes before finding the strength to move.

"Dear, are you okay?" Her mother wiped her hands on her apron before walking to Trudy to feel her forehead.

"Yes, Mother," Trudy sorrowfully returned to the porch, where she could leave her wet shoes.

Elsa continued with her kitchen chores when Trudy reentered the room.

"Sit, have cookies." Her mother motioned for the girl to take her chair at the table. Trudy did as she was told. Elsa contemplated how she should broach the subject of her daughter's obvious first crush. As she prepared a glass of milk, she played over in her mind what advice to give.

"You know, Trudy," she finally spoke, "I realize you are not a little girl anymore, and from this point forward, your actions will most likely be made as if you are an adult." She handed Trudy the milk and sat down across from her.

"Even adults sometimes don't make the right decisions when we let our emotions rule our heart. I never knew a time in my life without your father beside me. There was never a question of with whom I would spend the rest of my life. We have known everything about each other for our entire lives. It wasn't possible for there to be any surprises."

Elsa shifted uncomfortably in her chair.

"What I'm trying to say is that when *you* begin dating, you do not have that luxury. You need to guard your heart until you know who someone really is," she counseled. "Your father and I trust you completely. You have always made responsible decisions and we are proud of you."

Trudy bit into a butter cookie, searching her mother's eyes for any indication that she knew the truth.

Elsa did not seem to notice Trudy's apprehensiveness.

"Boys are not like girls," Elsa continued. "Girls want the fairy tale wedding and the perfect family from the moment they are old enough to pretend. Boys don't even begin to think about those things until they are grown men. They only want…" Elsa swallowed, trying to find the right words for such a delicate talk. "Boys have needs that are sometimes all consuming. When they are young, instead of the wedding and family, they just want the benefits that come with a marriage, without any of the responsibilities." Elsa, looked down at her hands, wondering if she was making herself clear.

Trudy continued to nibble, trying to keep her face as cool and undetectable as she could.

"Honey, do you understand what I'm trying to tell you? If a boy ever tells you he loves you and asks you to do anything more than to hold his hand, you have to tell him no. You have to remind yourself, that he doesn't want the same things you do. Otherwise, you might get badly hurt," she warned.

Trudy nodded her head as if agreeing. What she didn't want her mother to realize was that her words were too late. Trudy had already imagined her wedding, her house and, her family. Her mother may have been right about other couples, but she wasn't right about Trudy and Paul. Trudy already knew that she and Paul would be together forever.

CHAPTER NINE

I t felt like electric shocks were pulsing through Trudy's body all day Monday. She had spent another fitful and sleepless night, engrossed in her fantasy of what her next meeting with Paul would be like. He had not called Sunday. Maybe he didn't really like her, but was only being friendly. Trudy prayed repeatedly that he felt as she did.

During drama class, she waited for Miss Danton to mention Paul or their upcoming trip to Ashton, but she didn't. Trudy left class feeling as if she had dreamed the entire encounter with the love of her life. But hope sprung eternal.

"Maybe he will call me tonight," she told herself during Biology, English, and Algebra II. But then, her sabotaging mind would begin to fret over the idea that maybe the baseball game would be canceled because of the snow, although it had already melted away in the fifty-one degree temperatures of the day. For the rest of the day, there was no time that she could get comfortable. Her mind wretched with "what ifs," allowing no

room to process her teachers' lectures or assignments. Even at lunch, she couldn't eat. Her stomach was knotted with butterflies. The day was nothing short of miserable.

When she finally got home, she unloaded her books and went into the kitchen, seating herself at the old farm table.

"Hi Dear," her mother happily greeted her. "How was your day?"

Trudy mumbled something incoherent and her mother, distracted with rolling out a pie crust, didn't ask for clarification.

"There's some milk in the icebox," she told the girl, "and I think there is some Kringla too. Don't eat too many though; you'll spoil your dinner."

Trudy continued to sit, lost in her calculations of what time Paul might get home after baseball practice so that he could call. She knew that calling from Ashton might be a problem because of the long-distance charge. Phones, much less long distance calls were a luxury a lot of people around rural Oklahoma couldn't afford. She wondered if that might be the reason that Paul hadn't yet called her.

The idea gave her much needed comfort and she finally retrieved a glass from the cupboard and poured herself some milk. Seeing the Kringla made her realize how famished she was from missing lunch and she grabbed two of the doughy, sweet, pretzel shaped pastries.

After consuming them, Trudy sat awhile longer, watching her mother lay the crust into the glass pie pan and crimp the sides. Trudy could make pie crusts too, but they were never as pretty as Elsa's. Hers were too thick and made the crimp look more like a dent. She wondered if she should work on them in order to impress Paul.

As she finished her milk, Trudy contemplated a way to talk to her mother about the feelings of anxiousness, dread, elation, and joy that were surging through her body. She sighed and kept quiet, realizing from the things Elsa had told her the previous day, her mother probably wouldn't understand. So Trudy arose, got her books, and instead went to her room.

Trudy lay on her bed opening her history book to try once more to study for Tuesday's test. She read a couple of paragraphs before realizing, that while she had read the words, she hadn't comprehended them because she was too busy trying to decide what she should wear for her next meeting with Paul.

Her mother had just bought a very nice spring blouse with lilac flowers and matching lilac skirt for her, but it was probably too dressy for a baseball game. Depending upon the weather, she thought maybe she should wear her green plaid dress. It was much more casual. But then she thought that maybe she should wear her baby blue dress with the white collar so it would bring out the color in her eyes.

Trudy got up from her bed, almost in a panic. She had no idea what Paul would want to see her in and her frustration was starting to take her anxiousness to a whole new level. She even thought about calling Miss Danton to see what she was going to wear, before her better judgment prevailed. Trudy paced the floor, weighing all her options before returning to the blue dress.

"Paul did remark on my eyes," she reminded herself of their conversation Saturday night. *"The blue one it is."*

Trudy reluctantly ate dinner with her parents, hoping it would be interrupted by the ringing of the telephone. It wasn't. She bathed hurriedly, not wanting to miss the call if it came. It didn't. She joined her parents downstairs to listen to the *Ripley's Believe it or Not* radio show, again hoping it would be interrupted. She was left with only disappointment. Finally, she climbed into bed, and began torturing her own psyche.

He's already forgotten about me," she fretted. *"He really doesn't wasn't me to come to his game. He was only being nice. I'm sure that is why Miss Danton never mentioned it today,"* she lied to herself.

It wasn't long before her thoughts took a darker turn, and all the insults she had been subjected to in grade school and junior high came flooding back.

"I bet he only talked to me because Miss Danton made him because she feels sorry for me. He probably thought I was so ugly. I did look disgusting," Trudy told herself. *"I bet he heard the rumor about me with the football team and that is why he won't call. How could he possibly want to date me?"*

Trudy began to get angry. She hated those stupid girls at her school. They had already ruined most of her life and now they were trying to ruin the rest of it.

"I won't let them." She set her jaw. *"I will graduate as valedictorian of my class and I will go to school far away from here. I'll become a famous actress and they will regret that they ever bullied me,"* she planned. *"They will fall at my feet and beg forgiveness because they will be so jealous of who I am."*

Trudy took a deep breath and picked up her history book, trying yet again to study for her exam. After only a moment or two, she realized it was pointless. Her mind was only willing to focus on one thing. Her thoughts would not leave the boy who now had a permanent home in her heart.

CHAPTER TEN

T rudy dressed in her blue dress before bounding down the stairs to have breakfast with her mother and father. It seemed a good night's sleep had swept the demons of self-loathing from her memory, and she had awoken with a newfound hope for that day's meeting with Paul.

When she arrived at school, she literally counted the seconds of every class. At fourth period, when she had speech and drama, she hesitantly walked into the class with a gnawing in the back of her brain. Part of her expected Miss Danton to say that Paul had changed his mind about her coming to the game. The other part yearned for her teacher to pull her aside and make plans for that afternoon.

"Trudy, may I see you after class?" Miss Danton asked, as the students settled into the room.

Trudy nodded her head yes. She spent the hour on a roller coaster ride of emotions, wondering which scenario would confront her. The hour seemed to last three. Finally when the bell rang, she approached her teacher and waited for the verdict.

"Are you still planning on going with me to see Paul play?" Miss Danton asked her cheerily.

"Yes ma'am," Trudy answered.

"That's wonderful! We will have a great time. Why don't you meet me here in my room after school and we will get on the road."

Trudy was ecstatic. She walked on air the rest of the day, going to the bathroom between every class to check her makeup and hair. After what seemed an eternity of waiting, the final bell of the day rang, and Trudy once again checked her hair and makeup before going to meet Miss Danton.

Trudy put her school books in the back seat of Miss Danton's 1941 Ford and took a seat in the front. The two made small talk on the fifteen minute drive to Ashton. Trudy was dying to ask her teacher if Paul had said anything after they had dropped Trudy at home, but she couldn't bring herself to do so. She hoped that Miss Danton might volunteer the information on her own, but so far, she had not. Right before they pulled into the grass parking area south of the ball field, Miss Danton broke her silence on the subject.

"Paul is a very fine young man," she said to Trudy. "He's a wonderful student. He's kind to his parents. He's a good example to other kids and he will be successful at whatever he does."

Trudy nodded, devouring every word.

"I think you are the same way," Miss Danton smiled. "I am aware that you do not like to date, but I want to assure you that Paul is a good boy. You have to understand, just like you sometimes get consumed with drama, he gets consumed with baseball. Hopefully you both will find that you have a lot of things in common. If you do, you will need to be understanding of his time commitments, as he will have to be of yours."

Trudy again nodded her understanding before she, and her teacher, got out of the car and walked to the small set of bleachers behind home plate. Trudy took a seat next to Miss Danton, and before settling in, she spied her love.

Paul was behind third base with another player warming up his arm as the rest of the team tossed balls to their partners in the space between second, third, and the outfield fence.

Trudy couldn't take her eyes off the boy. She hoped he would look up and see her, and maybe wave, but he never looked away from his partner. She intently watched him studying the way each pitch hit his glove. When it was time for the game to begin, all of the team members ran into a huddle outside of their dugout and listened to last minute advice from their coach.

"Win!" she heard a husky voiced chorus chant before the group split – some taking the field as others filed into their cage. Paul walked calmly to the mound, turned and looked around the field. He pointed to the second baseman, telling him to back off the base a little more, before motioning to the center fielder to bring himself in a few more feet. He turned to look at his first baseman, smiled and then focused his attention on home plate and the first batter to step up to it.

Trudy's heart was beating out of her chest. She couldn't remember being this excited about anything, not even when she learned her father was building her a stage. She watched as Paul nodded to the catcher, and then lifted his left leg while tilting his body backwards. The ball, once cupped inside his strong hands, released at a speed so fast Trudy could barely even see it. She held her breath.

"Thump!" It hit the catcher's mitt.

"Strike!" the umpire yelled.

Several fans, including some high school girls who were huddled together on the far side of the bleachers, clapped and cheered.

"Way to go Paul!" a pretty brunette shouted.

"Do it again!" another girl said before the group collapsed into flirtatious giggles.

Trudy felt her face go red. The fact that Paul already had admirers was something she hadn't even considered. She felt a jealousy she had never known. She wanted to stand up and shout at them that Paul was hers, but at the same time, she realized how crazy it would sound considering she had only just met him. No one was going to understand the connection they had. She took a deep breath to calm herself before returning her eyes to the field.

"Strike!" she heard the umpire shout, although she had missed the actual pitch.

The girls shouted again. "Good job, Paul!"

Trudy's entire body went on alert. Who were these girls? Did Paul like one of them? Was she just here as a spectator and nothing more? Trudy wished like everything that Paul would at least look up and acknowledge her so she would know he really wanted her there.

"Strike!" she heard the umpire yell again and this caused the group of girls to jump up, clapping and whooping.

"Yay Paul!"

"You are great!"

"Swell!"

Trudy looked at Miss Danton to see if she was upset that these girls were so obviously flirting with her nephew, but her teacher hadn't even taken notice.

Trudy took another deep breath and waited for the next batter to take his stance.

Paul went through much of the same routine as before, nodding to his catcher, looking at the first baseman, and smiling before winding up his arm and letting the ball roar over the plate.

"Strike!" the umpire yelled. The batter backed out of the box and shook his head as if trying to clear it. He hit the ground a couple of times with the bat before stepping back in, bending his knees, and pulling his bat behind him, ready to swing.

Paul let the ball fly.

"Strike!"

The girls were now used to Paul striking out his opponents, and were busy chattering amongst themselves. Trudy relaxed a little.

Paul threw yet another strike followed by three strikes for the next batter. His teammates surrounded him as they left the field for their turn at bat. Trudy was beyond enamored.

Three batters preceded Paul. The first got a double. The second struck out and the third hit a single, sending the first batter to third.

Paul walked up the plate, took an assured stance and waited for the pitch.

The pitcher licked his lips before setting his jaw. He eyed Paul several seconds before turning to make sure the runner on first was not trying to steal second. When he was assured that the deuce base was safe, he turn back to Paul, and before Trudy had time to blink, he released the pitch.

A crack echoed through the field, as the ball headed high over second toward center field. It was hard for Trudy to see if the center fielder was going to catch it. He acted as if he was, but instead, the ball sailed over his head, coming to rest at the fence.

Paul sprinted like lightening toward first. He looked to center field to see that the player hadn't even made it to the fence to retrieve the ball. He rounded first and sprinted for second, dust flying from underneath his cleats.

The center fielder had reached the ball, but Paul put his speed to the test. He rounded second and accelerated toward the third bag. Paul looked at his coach who was motioning for him to stay on the base. He came to a screeching halt and turned to watch the ball sail to home plate. Then he grinned at his coach who congratulated Paul with a slap on the back.

Trudy couldn't contain her excited and jumped up and down in her seat, clapping madly.

The remainder of the game went much like the first inning. Paul only let two players on base, but both were stopped before they hit home plate.

Miss Danton leaned over to her student. "He's good, isn't he?" she asked Trudy.

"Oh my yes! He's wonderful," she dreamily sighed.

Trudy caught herself, and hoped Miss Danton hadn't heard the wistfulness in her voice. She knew if her teacher had, she would realize that Trudy thought Paul was wonderful in more areas than just baseball.

CHAPTER ELEVEN

A s soon as the game was over and the coach dismissed the team, Paul came over to the fence to face his aunt and Trudy.

"Didn't see your mom and dad here," Miss Danton said to him.

"Dad had to take some cattle to market in Stelter and Mom had to tend to a newborn colt," he answered before turning to Trudy and smiling.

Trudy felt electricity surge through her body.

"Hi Trudy." Paul grinned. "Thanks for coming. What did you think about the game?"

Trudy immediately became tongue tied. "Well, it was… you got them out, and you…," she looked at her hands searching for words that seemed to hide in the darkest recesses of her brain.

Paul laughed. "Yeah, I wish I could have gotten them all out. But those are the breaks."

"Paul, are you hungry? Maybe we could all go get a bite before we head back to Konawa. I'll take you home," Miss Danton said.

"I'd like that. The Diner is right down the road here. They have great pie." He looked to Trudy.

"Is that okay with you Trudy? Will your folks mind if we stay to eat supper?" Miss Danton asked her.

Trudy was ecstatic that she was going to get to spend time with Paul, and quite frankly, she didn't care if her parents minded, although she was sure they wouldn't.

"I'm sure it will be fine," she answered, smiling at Paul.

Paul grabbed his gear and met the two women at the car. He opened the passenger side door for Trudy and she blushed. Then he unloaded his gear into the back floorboard of the car and climbed in.

"How do you like your new car?" he leaned over the front seat and asked his aunt.

"It's been a little difficult learning to drive it, but so far, I'm very happy with it. I'm glad I saved the money Mother and

Daddy left me and bought it, especially since I'm now able to come see your games." She turned to her nephew and grinned.

Paul chuckled. "I'm glad you get to come to them too. I need all the support I can get," he humbled himself.

Trudy wanted so very much to tell him how amazing she thought he was, but she was afraid that she would stumble over her words as she had before.

The group made small talk on the five minute drive to The Diner. Again, Paul got out of the car and opened Trudy's door. Then he held the door to the restaurant open for her and his aunt.

The three ordered the blue plate special – roast beef, mashed potatoes, gravy, and green beans. They were also served big slabs of cornbread. Trudy picked at her food, too caught up in Paul's stories of the strategy he used against the day's opposing team. Although she didn't really understand much of what he was saying, she was enraptured never the less.

Paul took a big bite of the roast beef, coaxing it down with a gulp of milk. He wiped his face and then looked up at Trudy.

"I wanted to phone you," he said shyly, "but my parents say that the phone is for emergencies only."

Trudy nodded as the weight of the world lifted from her shoulders.

"I get to see my aunt every Sunday for dinner," he said, looking at Miss Danton, "Would it be okay if I send letters with her?"

Trudy lost her breath. She wanted to jump up and down in celebration, but managed to keep her composure.

"That would be nice." She shyly smiled.

Miss Danton, turned her head toward the window, trying not to show her own smile. She herself was not yet married, but she had been dating Mack Fields for almost a year and she knew it was only a matter of time. She still understood young love and there it was blossoming in front of her at that very moment.

The three finished their suppers. Paul grabbed the check before his aunt could.

"This is on me. I made some good money last summer hauling hay after we brought our own in," he semi-boasted. "I've managed to save the majority of it. It's been burning a hole in my pocket and I can't think of a better way to spend it," he said, looking Trudy in the eye.

Trudy was more than impressed and again, she blushed.

"Ready?" Paul asked the two women, after returning from paying their $2.25 tab. He helped Trudy and his aunt with their coats, and they reloaded themselves into Miss Danton's car.

"Well I wish I was going to be able to see your dad," Miss Danton told Paul, but your mom will have to do," she laughed.

Paul laughed too, because Miss Danton was his mother's sister and they were closer than any two people he knew.

Miss Danton took the two-lane road east – the same road that they had traveled to get to Ashton, but she turned north on a one lane gravel road about two miles outside of town. They traveled another two or three miles before Miss Danton turned east again onto a dirt drive. Trudy could see a large white farm house with a red barn about twenty yards off to its side. They both sat upon a small hillside. She looked around. There was a windmill to the south and a well and pump just about twenty feet to the south as well. She saw a fenced-in corral with a brown and white mare inside, and a few chickens roaming the yard. Then Trudy saw who she assumed was Paul's mother, exiting the barn to see who was coming up the drive.

As soon as his mother saw the car, she began waving and smiling. She hurried to it as Miss Danton, stilled the engine.

"Vera!" she hollered, opening her arms to hug her sister. "You got to see Paul play?"

"We did indeed Imogene!" Miss Danton answered.

Paul had once again opened Trudy's door and helped her out of the car. He cleared his throat.

"Mother, I'd like you to meet Trudy Dahl." He gently led Trudy around the front of the car toward his mother. Trudy hesitantly stuck out her hand.

"It's a pleasure to meet you Miss Dahl." Paul's mother smiled, shaking the girl's hand. "Are you all hungry?" she queried. "I can get supper started right away. Won't you stay?"

"Well I hope you don't mind, but Paul looked like he was famished after all his hard work on the ball field and we went to The Diner," Vera answered.

"Actually it's more than fine. Hollis thought he might just eat in Stelter before coming home, so this saves me from cooking. I could use the night off," she sighed. "The new foal is doing better, but I've been with him all day. I'm exhausted," she exhaled. "Won't you all come in for a moment?"

Miss Danton looked at Trudy. "Maybe we can stay for just a moment? I probably need to get Trudy back home soon."

Trudy tried to hide her excitement. "It's okay. We can stay a few more minutes."

The group walked to the old farmhouse. The women went inside while Paul and Trudy took a seat on the white porch swing.

"Thanks for coming to my game." Paul took Trudy's hand in his.

Trudy wanted to die. She had never been this happy.

"You're welcome." She tried hard not to let the exhilaration she felt show. "I really liked watching you pitch. You won the game for your team!"

"Oh no I didn't," Paul was quick to interject. "I just pitched. The rest of the team did all the work."

"Well, you didn't give them much work to do," Trudy giggled.

Paul blushed himself.

"I hope you will get to come to other games," he finally managed.

"I would really like that," she answered.

The two sat in silence for a few moments, pushing the swing with their feet. Trudy felt like she was in a dream.

Finally Paul spoke. "I'll send my first letter to you this Sunday. If you want, you can send one for me with my aunt. Maybe you can give it to her Friday?"

Trudy was so happy, knowing that Paul wanted to remain in touch. She could already think of a million things she wanted to tell him.

Miss Danton and Paul's mother opened the screen door as Paul pulled his hand quickly away from Trudy's.

"We better be getting along," Miss Danton said to Trudy.

Her teacher and Paul's mother hugged goodbye as Paul walked Trudy to the car. He opened her door and helped her in.

"I hope I see you soon Trudy Dahl," he smiled sweetly, his eyes giving away their joy. Then he closed the door and walked away.

CHAPTER TWELVE

D ear Paul, Trudy wrote before erasing it. Dearest Paul, she
tried again but erased it yet a second time.

Trudy lay on her bed contemplating the simple
greeting. Did Dear sound trite? Was Dearest too intimate? She
believed Paul felt as she did – that their love was destined for
greatness, the kind that would be talked about for ages to come.
However, she had been raised properly, and also suspected that
Miss Danton might spy, so she settled once again on Dear.

Dear Paul,

I so enjoyed your game. I hope
that I will be able to attend another
soon (if that is alright with you of
course). I also enjoyed our supper
together and our visit on your
porch.

How was the rest of your week?
I have a test in Algebra Thursday

and one in Biology on Friday so I have a lot of studying to do.

I liked your farm. We also have a barn but my father doesn't really farm, except for our vegetable garden. We also have chickens, two plow horses named Buttercup and Rufus and a milk cow named Ursula.

I hope someday you can come to my house. We have some wonderful woods behind our place. There is a big creek, called Jumper Creek, which runs through it.

Do you have any tests this week? How many students are in your class? There are seventy-two in mine. I hope to be Valedictorian.

I guess I should be going now so that I can begin to study. I will wait for your letter with great anticipation.

Sincerely yours,
Trudy

Trudy also anguished over the closing of her letter. Should she have put "Your friend?" What if it sent Paul the message that she only wanted to be friends? She certainly couldn't sign it "Love" although that is what she wanted to do more than anything. "Sincerely," seemed too business like. So, she opted for "Sincerely yours," hoping that Paul would realize she was sincerely his, but wanting Miss Danton to think she was being proper and innocuous.

Trudy spritzed the pink paper with Lavender perfume before folding it, and sealing it inside its matching envelope. She carefully, and with her best penmanship, wrote "PAUL" on the front. She then stuck the letter into her notebook.

Trudy wondered when to deliver the letter to Miss Danton. She did not want to risk giving the letter to her immediately following class because she didn't want any of the students seeing her. She wanted to keep the magical relationship all to herself. It was bad enough that Miss Danton needed to know. She hoped her teacher wouldn't tell anyone else. She decided she would give it to Paul's aunt immediately following school on Friday.

Again the days seemed to slow as if some cosmic time machine was ordering minutes to elapse at the speed of hours, and hours to elapse like days. Friday took a month to come, and the Sunday when Trudy knew her letter would be delivered, seemed to hide its existence from the world.

That entire day she second guessed each word she had put onto paper. Did she sound too anxious? Did she sound too uninterested? Trudy was in agony, wishing she could magically bring the letter back and rework it. She fretted so much, she actually made herself sick, and when her mother called for her to come to dinner, she knew she would not be able to eat.

"I'm not feeling well," she told her mother. "I don't want dinner."

Elsa felt Trudy's forehead, declaring she had no fever, but never the less excused her daughter from the dinner table. Trudy retreated back to her room, throwing herself onto her bed to rehash – yet again – what she deemed would be the end of her budding relationship.

"He will think I don't like him," she told herself one moment, before deciding that Paul would think she was too boring, or forward, or juvenile, the next. The rest of the night was spent imagining every reaction her soulmate could have, and none of them were good. Finally Trudy fell asleep where she lay, fully clothed, without washing her face or brushing her teeth.

At morning's light, she awoke. A sick foreboding had nestled into the recesses of her stomach. Today she would receive Paul's reply. Today would be the day her love would be dashed. Today would be the beginning of the end of her life.

Trudy dressed for school, again told her mother she was not able to eat, and walked outside to wait for the school bus.

As if mimicking earlier days, time toyed with her, making the hours before her drama class as strange and fantastical as her favorite book, *The Adventures of Alice in Wonderland.* One moment, while she was in the throes of dread, the seconds would rush to complete their circular rotation around the clock. In moments of hope, they would stall, refusing to move ahead. Trudy thought she was going crazy.

When the third period bell rang, Trudy reluctantly left her class and walked slowly to Miss Danton's room. She took her seat, not removing her eyes from Paul's aunt. Miss Danton, however, never even made eye contact with Trudy. Instead she kept her head buried in her planner, mumbling to herself while jotting notes.

Again time warped, ebbing and flowing throughout the class, as Miss Danton discussed the final two months of the school year, and the expectations she had for a regional speech and debate competition.

"Class, I've entered you in the Wrenville Regionals," she revealed. "We have a lot of work to do to prepare, but I have full confidence that you all can bring home superiors. And," she added while looking directly at Trudy, "my guess is that there are many that could advance to state."

Hearing of Miss Danton's plans was not the good news it would have normally been for Trudy. She didn't want to participate. She felt as though it was now a waste of time, as she had found better ways to spend hers.

First and foremost, she could spend it trying to find a way to get Paul to see that she wasn't as pathetic as her letter made her sound. She wasn't sure how she would accomplish it, but she needed every moment of her spare time to figure it out.

Finally the period bell sounded and Trudy began to rise. She stood looking at Miss Danton, waiting for her to ask Trudy to stay behind, but she didn't. Trudy's worst nightmare was confirmed. Paul wasn't going to answer the ridiculous letter she had written to him. Why would he? Trudy left the room, head buried, but swimming, with the confirmed knowledge her dreams were over.

A few steps before Trudy reached her locker, someone pulled on her shoulder. Trudy spun around.

"Trudy," Miss Danton was breathless, "oh my, I forgot to give you this, so I had to run after you," she laughed. "Paul sent this to you and he wanted me to ask you if you might want to attend another game. The boys play again Thursday."

Trudy exhaled as if she had been holding her breath for days, which she felt like she actually had.

"Oh yes! I would love to!"

"Well, they actually aren't playing in Ashton this time, but Lithia. It's only about ten minutes further. Do you think your parents would mind?"

"I'll ask, but I don't think so," she answered. "I will let you know for sure tomorrow." Trudy was giddy.

Most of the kids had already moved toward the cafeteria for lunch period. Trudy opened her locker and used the door to shield her from the stragglers still making their way through the hall. She ripped into the plain white envelope.

Dear Trudy,

I was very excited to receive your letter Sunday. I couldn't wait to read it, but I had to because my family was ready to have dinner – ha.

As soon as we finished, I opened it. I'm really glad that you liked the game. Of course it is alright with me if you attend others. I would love it if you came to all my games. In fact, I asked my aunt to see if you might want to come to the game in Lithia this coming Thursday. We played again last Thursday but it was in Stelter and my aunt wasn't able to drive that far, so I figured you wouldn't be able to go either. By the way, we beat them 4 to 1! I didn't have as many strikeouts as I had on Tuesday.

We too have a lot of farm animals. I like the names you have given yours. Our milk cow is Miss Molly. Our plow horses are Tillie and Stuart. We also have a goat named Buster and one named Bitsy. We have a mule named Hoss and believe it or not, I even have a chicken named Ruffles because her feathers are a lot fluffier than our other chickens. She is my favorite.

Your house sounds really neat. I love the woods. We have them here too, although they are on the other side of the hill from where our house sits. I have seen both a bobcat and a cougar there. Have you ever seen those at your place? Of course we have a lot of coyotes too.

I once had a pet barn owl named Mortimer. He had hurt his wing and couldn't fly very well. He was afraid of thunderstorms! One day, when it thundered he tried to fly underneath the chicken coop and he hit his head and died. I was really sad about it.

I have a Chemistry test Monday. I've spent most of the weekend, when I wasn't doing chores, studying for it. I think I'm prepared. By the time you read this, I will have already taken the test, or I would ask you to wish me luck.

We only have forty-five in our class. We are all very close, almost like siblings – ha. We've all gone to school together since first grade. Is it like that in Konawa?

Well, I guess I ought to close for now. I still need to study, and my aunt is getting ready to leave, so I better give this to her so that she can give it to you. I hope you can come Thursday. I think you are good luck for me!

Sincerely yours,
Paul

T rudy squealed in her head. "He said I was good luck for him! I can't believe it! He must really like me; he wrote four whole pages!"

Trudy didn't know what to do with herself. She knew she needed to go to the cafeteria. She hadn't eaten since noon the day before. She stuck the letter into her binder and tucked it safely away in her locker. She dreamily walked down the hall to have lunch. Her head swam with all the new information Paul had shared with her.

"Miss Molly – that's precious," she thought. *"Bitsy and Buster, what cute names. A chicken named Ruffles?"* Trudy hoped she would get to see it. *"Hoss is a good name for a mule,"* she mused. *"Stuart and Tillie, those are perfect farm names for horses. They are solid and endearing,"* she analyzed.

Trudy found herself with a tray and already seated before

she even realized she was in the cafeteria. She sat by herself in the corner, hoping not to have her thoughts interrupted.

"Dad once said he saw a cougar in back by the caves near the creek," she remembered. *"I will have to tell Paul that. I don't think we ever had a bobcat, but I will ask. Oh I can't wait to go to Lithia!"* Trudy jumped a little with excitement. *"I hope Mother and Daddy will let me."*

Trudy detailed just what she would say to her parents to gain their permission. First she would tell them that she had all her studies for the week done – and she would by cramming for the next three nights. Then she would tell them that Miss Danton had personally asked for Trudy to be her escort so she wouldn't have to drive alone. Then she would play on her Dad's love of the game, telling him that she too was becoming interested in it.

Trudy sighed. She hoped more than anything that it would work. She couldn't bear it if she didn't get to see Paul again.

"Um, Miss Danton asked if I might be able to accompany her to her nephew's game in Lithia this Thursday after school," she broached at the dinner table that night.

Before her parents could answer, she told them of her studies and her new found love of the game. Knute and Elsa looked at each other, both fully realizing the ploy playing out in front of them.

"Well Honey," Knute began, "I'm very happy that you are beginning to appreciate the game, but Thursday is a school night."

Trudy started to protest but Knute held up his hand for her to let him finish.

"Ashton is only fifteen minutes from here. Lithia is twice that far. You got in pretty late from the Ashton game. I wouldn't want you to get in that late again."

Barely able to contain herself, Trudy blurted out."Oh no, see we went to eat after the game in Ashton and we had to drop her nephew off at his home, and Miss Danton wanted to visit with her sister. We won't be doing any of that this time. Paul has to ride home with the team."

Trudy pleaded her case not only with her mouth but her hands, face and eyes. "Please Dad," she twisted her face, wrung her hands and batted her eyelashes, trying to use the power only a daddy's girl has.

Knute looked at Elsa. "What do you think Mother?"

Elsa cleared her throat, wanting Trudy to realize that they were not just going to cave because of her admirable manipulations.

"I don't know. Like your father said, it's a school night and this is twice in two weeks," she unapologetically stated.

Trudy's chin hit her chest as if she had been delivered a fatal blow. Elsa secretly smiled, seeing that her daughter was deep in the middle of a full-blown love affair.

"Mother, please. It won't become a habit. I really need some time to do a few things I want to do. I'm always studying. I'm always doing rehearsals. I'm always getting ready for scholastic meets. I really try to make you and Dad proud. Please let me have this."

Elsa had to agree that Trudy worked very hard to make them proud. She had never been in trouble, except for the notes that had been sent home when she was younger. But she had obviously long outgrown those issues.

Elsa looked again at Knute, as if asking if it was okay with him. Apparently Trudy's reminder of her accomplishments served to change his mind as well, and he nodded to his wife.

"Okay," Elsa sighed, "but don't stay out as late."

Trudy squealed and jumped up from her seat. "May I be excused?" she asked.

"Trudy, you haven't touched your dinner. You have to eat, so sit back down and at least have a bite." Elsa pointed to Trudy's chair.

Trudy slunk back down and hurriedly piled potatoes, peas, and pork steak, into her mouth. In less than five minutes, she asked again. "May I be excused?"

"Don't you want pie?" her mother asked.

"No ma'am," Trudy answered.

"Okay then, you are excused," Elsa replied.

Trudy ran upstairs, grabbed paper from her desk and jumped onto her bed. She took her Algebra II book and used it as a desk.

Dear Paul,

I love the names you have given your animals! They are so perfect. I also have a dog named Maxwell and a cat named Teddy. Do you have a dog or cat? I didn't see any when I was at your house.

As you will see, I will give you this letter after your game

Thursday. I can't wait to see you play again. I hope that I am good luck for you and that your team will win.

How did your test go? I got A's on both of mine. Luckily I don't have any this week. Your aunt has entered us in a speech and debate contest in Wrenville in a few weeks so we are trying to get ready for it. I am doing a dramatic prose from "Their Eyes Were Watching God," by Zora Neale Hurston. It is a very new book, and was just published a few years ago, but it is one of my all-time favorites.

Trudy hoped Paul might look into the book. If he did, he would find that it was a Southern love story. And although the circumstances were different, at least he might see that she had planned her selection because of him and because, she herself, was in love.

Miss Danton has asked me to also compete with Michael Allen in a humorous duet from "Our Gang." We will have to stay after school a few times in order to prepare properly.

I can't believe you have seen both a bobcat and a cougar. I remember my Dad telling us that he had seen a cougar, but I don't believe we have had any bobcats. I think I would be scared if I saw either!

I think it is neat that you had a barn owl. Owls are so cute. I wish I could have one for a pet. I also wish I could have met Mortimer. I'm sorry that he died.

I don't think our class is as close as yours. We have had a lot of kids move here just in high school. We have also had many move away. I have gone to school here since first grade and several others have too, but there are just as many who haven't.

Well I guess I will go now. I too have a lot of studying and work. I'm going to try and finish all this week's assignments by Wednesday so that I will have nothing to worry about on Thursday (except your game of course — ha)!

Sincerely yours,
Trudy

Trudy again spritzed the three pages of her letter and placed them inside the envelope. She sighed. The day had been one of the best of her life.

CHAPTER FOURTEEN

T rudy worked feverishly to get all the week's assignments completed. She also asked Michael Allen if he would be willing to stay after school all three days, to practice their competition piece, so that she could take off Thursday and hopefully Friday. He obliged. The busyness of her days made her thankful because time passed quickly.

Thursday morning she dressed in the green plaid dress that she had debated on wearing to Paul's first game. She also brought a light sweater in case the temperatures dropped.

March had turned into April and although the threat of snow had passed, Oklahoma was now embarking on Tornado Season. The state song "Oklahoma" was correct in that "the winds come sweeping down the plains." It was incorrect in, that most of the time, they did more than sweep. They usually blustered, and because the jet streams were hit and miss as to from which direction they would come, it could still be quite chilly.

Again, Trudy met Miss Danton after school and the two hit the road for the thirty-five minute drive to Lithia. They talked about the upcoming contest. Miss Danton told Trudy she felt as though if she continued on her acting path, she might be able to get a scholarship to college.

Trudy was happy to hear the news but she was no longer sure if it was the path in life she wanted to take. Wife and mother sounded like the perfect life for her, but only if she could be a wife to Paul, and the mother of his children.

When Trudy and Miss Danton arrived at the game, they were met by Paul's parents. Miss Danton introduced Trudy to Paul's father, Hollis. It was clear where Paul got his good looks. The man was a tall, and strong. He had a squared jawline, the same blue eyes as Paul's, and although his hair was graying, it served only to make him more distinguished.

Trudy and her teacher sat next to Paul's folks. The game immediately was much quieter than the last, as there were no girls in the stands cheering for Paul. Miss Danton and Paul's mother talked throughout most of the game. Trudy overheard some conversation of an upcoming wedding, but didn't know whose.

Paul allowed only two hits in the game. One was a bunt, which Paul quickly recovered and used to tag the batter out, and the other headed straight for the shortstop, who bobbled the catch and allowed the runner to get safely to first.

Paul didn't allow anyone else on base so Lithia remained scoreless. Ashton however had four great hits. Two had come from Paul and one from the third baseman – all triples. Ashton's first baseman also had a home run. The final score was six to nothing.

The players filed off the field after shaking hands and regrouped in their respective dugouts. Trudy sat anxiously, wondering if she would get a chance to speak to Paul privately. Both his parents and his aunt remained seated on the bleachers, so Trudy assumed that they too might be waiting for Paul to speak to them. It wasn't long before members of the team, who had relatives watching them, did in fact, come to the bleachers to say hello.

"Great game Son," Paul's father said as the boy ambled over to the seats.

"It certainly was," his mother agreed.

"Paul if you get any better, I think you may have to sign up for the pros," his aunt chuckled.

"How are the wedding plans going?" Paul playfully punched his aunt in the shoulder.

"We are on track for a fall wedding," she happily announced.

"That's great. I bet we could get some of the farm animals to be witnesses," he teased. The group laughed.

Paul smiled at them all before turning his attention toward Trudy.

"Hi," he shyly grinned. "Thanks for coming." Paul kicked the dirt beneath his feet, obviously a little embarrassed that his conversation with Trudy would be overheard by his family.

"You were great again," Trudy responded, blushing a little herself.

"It's too bad we can't have supper again tonight." He shrugged his shoulders. "Coach likes us to ride back as a team though."

"That's okay, my mom and dad want me home early tonight," Trudy replied.

Paul stepped up the two bleacher seats to sit beside Trudy.

"Do you have something for me?" he asked.

At first Trudy panicked. Did he want her to kiss him right then and there with *everybody* watching? She almost lost her breath at the thought of her lips meeting his.

Paul saw that Trudy was confused and reminded her of the letter she promised. Trudy exhaled with her own relief, at the same time that the butterflies that had been alighting in her stomach, dove to stillness. She pulled the envelope from her pocket and handed it to Paul.

"Will you send a reply with your aunt on Sunday?" she hoped aloud.

"Sure," Paul answered. "I'm really enjoying learning more about you."

"Let's go boys!" Paul's coach yelled from the dugout.

"I've got to get going. Oh, by the way, I have another away game on Tuesday..." he grinned like the Cheshire Cat, "at Konawa."

Trudy's mouth hit the floor. "Really?" Her eyes revealed her complete joy.

"At four. Just in time for you to get out of school and come watch. Will you be there?"

"Yes." Trudy smiled, biting her lower lip. "I will."

"Okay, I'll see you then," Paul said as he arose to leave. "Will you pick me up at the school?" he asked his parents over his shoulder as he ventured toward his coach.

"We're following the bus," his father answered.

On the ride home, Trudy was lost in her own thoughts, remaining silent for several miles. Although at first she was ecstatic that Paul would be coming to Konawa, the reality of the situation set in. She had never before attended a Konawa baseball game. It would be odd for her to do so now and people were going to talk. Also, her father did attend the games, so there was going to be no way to avoid having him meet Paul.

"Penny for your thoughts." Miss Danton interrupted her contemplation.

"I'm just wondering if I can really go Paul's game Tuesday," Trudy confessed.

"Why in the world not?" Miss Danton questioned. "After all there's no traveling involved."

"I don't really want the other students knowing," Trudy buried her head.

Miss Danton sat in silence for a while before answering.

"Trudy, let me ask you something."

Trudy nodded her head.

"What are you afraid of?"

Trudy thought about the question a moment. What was she afraid of? Would the kids make fun of her? Would they taunt her? Would they start rumors? What if her dad didn't like Paul and forbid her from seeing him? Were these the things that were making her hesitant?

Although each one in itself was a good enough reason to be afraid, none of them was *the* reason. Trudy realized the real reason she was afraid was because she didn't want anyone to judge what was happening between Paul and her. She didn't want the same immature students – who had made her life miserable – to sully the beauty of their transcendent relationship. She knew there was no one on the planet, especially her classmates, who could understand the magnitude of their love. She wasn't about to let the outsiders define what there was no way to define. Those people had spent years taking from her – her dignity, her beauty, her self-confidence and her self-worth. She was not about to let them take the thing that mattered more than any of those – the *only* thing that mattered her.

Trudy finally answered her teacher, but not with the truth. "Nothing, I guess," she lied.

"Well good, because you can't worry about what anyone else thinks," Miss Danton answered, as if she had read Trudy's mind. "Look at me Trudy," she continued. "A lot of people told me I should put 'silly notions' like going to college instead of getting married, out of my head. They said I'd be an old spinster if I didn't. But they were wrong," she looked at Trudy.

It was then that Paul's joking at the baseball field finally sunk in. Trudy had been so consumed with seeing Paul that the conversation hadn't registered.

"You're getting married!" she gasped.

Miss Danton laughed. "I am. However, it's not common knowledge yet so I hope you will not repeat it to anyone."

"Oh I won't I promise." Trudy clapped her hands. "How did it happen? How did he propose?"

Miss Danton blushed, weighing if it was appropriate to discuss such issues with a student, but her own excitement won out.

"It was magical," she surreally smiled. "He took me to that wonderful dinner club in Maiden," she recalled. "After we had dinner, he asked if I would like to take a walk around Wintervail Park. When we were walking across the big bridge, he stopped in the middle of it. He took me by the hands and told me how much he loved me. Then he took a knee, pulled a box from his pocket and asked if I would marry him," she sighed, lost in the memory of the evening.

"That's so romantic," Trudy sighed too.

"I think so," Miss Danton smiled. "I wouldn't have wanted it to be any different."

Trudy again became lost in her own thoughts. Unlike Miss Danton, she didn't think she could wait so many years after high school to marry Paul. Hopefully their life together would begin the moment they graduated.

CHAPTER FIFTEEN

The weekend was again, excruciatingly long as Trudy counted the moments to Monday's drama class and the letter that awaited her. This time Miss Danton didn't forget to give her the letter. Trudy rushed to her locker, and awaited the moment the hall was empty so she could read it.

Dear Trudy,

It was great to see you at my game again. See I was right; you are good luck for me! I hope you still like coming to my games and I'm very excited to see you Tuesday. I imagine it will be hard for you to watch since you go to school there. I hope you won't be too upset if we win, although I hear Konawa is pretty good this year.

I don't think I told you that I play basketball too. I like the game okay but baseball is my favorite. I hope to be able to play in the big leagues. I think my folks would like me to go on to college and play there first, but if I got the chance to even go to the minors first, I think I would do that. A lot of the time, a minor league career can lead to the majors. I love the St. Louis Cardinals. If I got my wish, that is who I would play for. I hope I could be as good as Dizzy Dean was when he pitched for them, especially during the '34 season.

I've also toyed with the idea of going into the army to help with this war. Dad says by the time I graduate, it will be over. If that is the case, I would rather go to on and play ball.

We have a dog too. Her name is Blackie. She's an old mutt that came up one winter. She was half starved to death. She's a good girl and she goes with me to do my chores and keeps me company. We have several cats. Dad keeps them in the barn as mousers. My favorite one is Boo Kitty. We named her that because she is black as midnight —ha. She talks all the time. She meows and meows like she is carrying on an entire conversation with you.

I got a 92 on my Chemistry test, so it was an A. I have a Geography test Tuesday before the game. Luckily it is third hour so I'll be through with it by the time I pitch. I don't like to have those things hanging over my head when I'm on the mound.

Your speech competition sounds like a lot of work. I know you will do great though. You were really good in the play. My aunt said you are the best student she has ever had and I know she wouldn't lie to me — ha. You will have to let me know if you perform anymore at your school this year so I can come and see you again.

Well I still have some chores to take care of and more studying. I'm glad I will get to see you Tuesday.

Sincerely yours,
Paul

Trudy finished reading but couldn't tear herself away, so she reread the letter quickly before rushing to the cafeteria. She again sat in the corner, immersed in her thoughts about the newest correspondence.

"He talked a lot about baseball," she mused. *"He didn't say anything about getting married after school. He probably just assumes that I'll go with him. And, of course I will."* She happily smiled to herself.

Trudy spent the rest of the day on auto-pilot. She continued to be torn between wanting to see her beloved again, and not wanting others to know of their relationship. She had already gotten the nerve to tell her father she would be at the game. He and her mother had reacted very reasonably.

"Well I'm glad I will finally get to meet this young man in person," he told his daughter. He also asked Elsa if she would like to join them so she too could meet the boy who had captured Trudy's heart. Although Elsa usually wasn't one to go a game, she readily agreed.

"I think it would be nice for us to go as a family," she had answered.

The idea that Trudy would be with her folks actually gave her a little comfort. Maybe the other students wouldn't think it was so odd for her to be there if she were with her parents. In the meantime, all she could do was hope that most of the other students cleared out before Paul came to meet her, and introductions were made. The thought sent butterflies through her stomach.

Trudy left her parents at the kitchen table and went upstairs to respond to Paul's letter.

Dear Paul,

I wish I knew who Dizzy Dean was but I don't. I know I've heard my father talk about him. He must be really good. I think it would be wonderful for you to play in the big leagues, but I understand your parents wanting you to go to college first.

I don't know what I want to do after high school. I think I will keep it open for a while before deciding.

I'm excited for your game tomorrow. I won't be upset if your team wins. I understand someone has to lose. I hope you won't be upset if Konawa wins — ha.

I can't believe Miss Danton thinks I'm the best student she has ever had. That is really neat. I like her very much. I'm so excited that she is getting married. I bet they will have a beautiful wedding. I love weddings, don't you?

I won't have any other plays this year - only our speech competition. I am happy that everything is winding down for the end of school. I really love summer. I like to swim and I love all the newborn animals. By the time I'm out of school, they are the perfect size to play with. Do you get a lot of new animals in the spring?

I guess I better be going now. Mother has asked me to help with supper. I will see you tomorrow at the game.

Sincerely yours,
Trudy

Tuesday played the same tricks on her as the Monday when she had awaited Paul's first letter. It slowed when she was anxious to see Paul, and sped when she became leery of the consequences.

When the final bell rang, she slowly walked to her locker, her stomach both queasy and excited. She took the books she would need for her evening studies, put on her favorite light sweater and walked to the field.

"Trudy!" she heard Miss Danton yell behind her.

Trudy turned and saw her teacher hailing her. "Wait up and I'll walk with you."

When they reached the field, Trudy's parents were already there. Trudy reintroduced them to her teacher.

"We appreciate you taking Trudy with you to your nephew's games," her mother said.

"Oh not at all," Miss Danton smiled. "I love the company. I try to go to as many of his games as I can, but I can usually only make the ones that aren't too far away. I know the drives aren't long, but it is nice to have someone to talk to." She looked at Trudy.

"Won't you have a seat with us?" Knute asked, as he motioned for her to sit by Elsa.

"I'd love to, but my sister and brother-in-law should be getting here any moment to watch Paul. I usually sit with them so that I can put in my two-cents worth," she chuckled.

Knute and Elsa nodded.

"Have a seat, Sweetie." Elsa motioned to Trudy.

Trudy did as she was told. The butterflies in her stomach went to town. Trudy hadn't even thought about the idea that her mother and father would also be meeting Paul's mother and father. She hoped they would like each other.

Paul's parents arrived at the exact time Trudy was wondering how the couples would interact. Miss Danton hugged Paul's mother and teasingly slapped his father on the arm. She led them over to where Trudy and her parents were sitting.

"Mr. and Mrs. Dahl, this is my sister, Imogene and her husband Hollis. These are Trudy's parents," she told her relatives.

The group exchanged pleasantries before Paul's family took a seat directly in front of the Dahls. A conversation between the two men quickly ensued.

"I heard your boy is a great pitcher," Knute said to Hollis.

Hollis turned to look at the man paying the compliment.

"That's what they tell me, but I wouldn't really know. I never played the game. I played football," he answered.

"I played football too, but I also played baseball. If he's half as good as our coaches have been saying, then you may have a pro player on your hands," Knute assured the man.

"Oh I don't know about that," Hollis smiled, obviously proud, "Making it to the pros is a one in a million kind of thing. I'm sure there are plenty of good players out there ready for their own shot," he humbly replied.

"Well I can't wait to see what he's got." Knute slapped Paul's father on the back. "I've been looking forward to it all season."

Trudy smiled to herself. It couldn't have gone any better.

The game went very much like the others Trudy had seen, with a couple of exceptions. Konawa was clearly stronger than the other teams she had seen play against Ashton. They also had a really good third baseman, Lee Bland. Lee, who was over six foot tall, jumped like he had springs for legs, and caught a soaring fly headed for left field. It just so happened that ball was Paul's and he was out on his first bat. Had it been anyone else besides Tom at that position, the ball would have probably hit the fence. His next time at bat, Paul adjusted his swing to send the ball past the shortstop and between the left and center fielder. He landed himself a triple, sending one batter home.

The other exception was that Konawa had two power hitters. Bland shared the honors with the center fielder, Vern Paxton. Paxton had the game's only home run and Bland batted triples twice.

As far as Paul's pitching went, it would have been flawless was it not for the strong batting lineup of his competition. He only allowed two other players a hit. Unfortunately they were the ones on base before Bland and Paxton took their turns.

Konawa had what normally would have been considered a good pitcher, but in comparison to Paul Somerton, Will Roberts was only above average.

Although Roberts only allowed two hits in the fourth, and three in the sixth and seventh innings, those proved to be the Konawa Tigers' demise. The game ended with Ashton winning it five to four.

Only a few students had actually shown up for the game and most of them had a brother playing. They hung around the back of the stands a few moments after the game, but left rather quickly. Paul was still in the dugout with his team when the coast became clear. Trudy waited anxiously for him to arrive.

Paul shook hands with a few of his fellow players before walking toward the group that had assembled to watch him.

"Another good one, Son," his dad said, as he patted the boy on the back.

"We are really proud of you," his mother beamed.

"Paul, I'm not the only one who thinks you might go pro," Miss Danton laughed, while pointing to Trudy's dad.

"This is Trudy's father, Knute Dahl, and her mother Elsa Dahl."

"You had a good game there young man." Knute nodded to him.

"It's nice to meet you Sir, Ma'am," he said, looking to Trudy's parents. "That's awfully nice of you to say. Konawa is the hardest team we've played all year. I wasn't sure we were going to pull it out."

"We do have some good players," Knute agreed, "but the pitching is what won this one. I heard you were good, and they were right."

Trudy almost couldn't contain her excitement. She never imagined that the meeting would go so well. She was smiling when Paul caught her eye.

"Do you mind if I have a word with your daughter?" he asked Knute, although he never took his eyes off Trudy.

Knute looked at Elsa, who slightly shook her head.

"You may," Knute answered.

Paul walked toward Trudy and led her to the side of the bleachers.

"Well, what did you think? Are you upset that Konawa lost?"

"No," Trudy bit her lower lip. "I'm glad you won. You played a great game. My dad thinks you are really good. He loves baseball, so he knows what he is talking about." She shrugged her shoulders.

"That's nice of him," Paul replied. "I can't take the credit though. I've got a great team. They don't lose their focus. I never have to worry that they are going to let something get by them. It makes my job easier."

Ashton's coach put out the call that the team needed to reassemble in order to leave.

Trudy looked panicked. She and Paul had only gotten a few seconds together. Paul leaned in and whispered in her ear. "You got something for me?"

This time Trudy knew he meant the letter and she took it from her purse and handed it to him.

"By the way, my aunt and her fiancé are coming to get me Friday for the picture show. I'd like to ask your parents if you can go with us. Is that okay?"

Trudy almost jumped with excitement, but managed to stay calm. "Yes," she answered, but Paul was already walking toward her father.

"My aunt and her fiancé are going to take me to the picture show in Maiden Friday night. I was wondering if Trudy could come with us?"

Knute felt as if his head was on fire. He had always thought he would be ready for this day, but he wasn't. His only daughter was about to begin dating and it caused every cell in his body to scream in anguish. She was still his baby and he wanted more than anything to say no, but, he knew he couldn't.

"If you don't mind, let her mother and I discuss it and Trudy can tell Miss Danton tomorrow," he stalled.

Paul's parents, both shifted their stance, obviously as uncomfortable as Knute.

"Yes sir," Paul answered. "Thank you for considering it." He shook Knute's hand.

"Mom, Dad, I've got to get going. I'll see you at home," he smiled. They smiled back.

Trudy watched Paul load the bus with his teammates. She walked to her parent's car with them, but she had no memory of the ride home. All she could think about was the proposed first date.

CHAPTER SIXTEEN

T rudy waited anxiously during dinner for her parents to address the date issue. She shifted impatiently back and forth in her seat, wanting to get the conversation started, but not wanting Knute and Elsa to know how eager she was. Trudy felt the butterflies grow inside her stomach. She knew her happiness for the rest of her life depended on the decision her parents would make. She prayed that their answer would be the one to make her dreams come true. Her anxiety increased when, by the time dinner was over, it had not been mentioned.

Elsa arose and began clearing the table. Trudy remained seated glancing back and forth between her father and mother, and silently willing them to open the subject for conversation. They both seemed oblivious to her pleading stares. Finally, she arose herself and saddled up beside her mother at the kitchen sink.

"Have you and Dad decided if I can go to the picture show with Miss Danton and Paul?" she quietly asked.

Her mother stopped washing the glass in her hand and turned to look at Trudy.

"We need some time to think this over, Trudy," she shrugged. "Give us until the morning okay?"

Trudy wanted to scream. They were treating her like a baby. She should have been dating at least a year ago. They should have already decided about her dating age long ago. It wasn't fair.

"Mother, I'm sixteen. I'll be seventeen in September. I should be allowed to go out by now. Annnnd..." she emphasized, "we are not even going by ourselves. There will be two adults with us. You can't possibly have any objection with that," Trudy huffed.

"You make very good points, Trudy," her mother admitted. "I promise you that your father and I will put all that into the mix. But, it is our job to make sure we protect you and make the right decisions for you. I'm sure Paul is a very nice young man, but we need to at least discuss it."

Then she leaned closely into her daughter and whispered into her ear. "I'm sure you have nothing to worry about."

Trudy looked at her mother, who winked.

Trudy smiled and almost did a little shimmy, but caught herself before her father could see. She hurriedly helped her mother clean the rest of the kitchen before calmly walking up the stairs to her room. As soon as she entered and closed the door behind her, she let out a silent but ecstatic scream and released the shimmy she had repressed earlier. Then she began ripping through her closet to find the perfect first date outfit.

Trudy settled on a plum cardigan set and ivory and plum stripped skirt. She bathed and readied herself for bed. As she lay in the quiet, her mother knocked on her door.

"Come in," Trudy answered the knock.

Her mother entered and sat on the side of the bed next to her beautiful daughter.

"Your father and I talked. We are going to allow you to go to Maiden with Paul." Elsa's smile gave away her own joy.

Trudy hugged her mother as if she would never let her go. Elsa laughed.

"Wow, is that what I have to do now to get a hug like that?" she teased. Trudy hugged her even tighter.

"We would like to get to know Paul a little better," her mother said as the hug continued. Trudy broke the embrace.

133

"You're not going with us are you?" Trudy couldn't hide the panic in her eyes.

"No Honey," her mother laughed. "We would like you to invite Paul over for Sunday dinner after church. Your father can pick him up while you and I get the food ready."

"Oh yes!" Trudy grinned from ear to ear. "That would be great. I will ask him Friday night."

After Elsa left, Trudy tried to sleep, but her excitement wouldn't allow it. She couldn't wait for Friday. She couldn't wait for Sunday. She replayed every scenario she could think of between her true love and herself. Would he hold her hand in front of his aunt and future uncle? Might he even put his arm around her? Was there any way he would be able to kiss her?

She couldn't conjure a way for the kiss to take place, although she tried for what seemed hours. What would they all do on Sunday after dinner? She hoped that maybe she would be allowed to show Paul around the property. If she could, and they were able to amble through the woods or go to the pond, she knew he would have the perfect opportunity to kiss her.

She imagined the kiss. Paul had beautiful, full lips. She closed her eyes and felt them meet hers. The thought was glorious. She couldn't wait for Sunday. She knew her parents would love Paul as much as she did. They would have to. After all, he was going to be their son-in-law wasn't he?

Friday evening finally arrived and Trudy was the happiest she had ever remembered being. She knew she was in love. She hoped Paul was too. She floated through the day, and even after she got home while she dressed. She applied a small amount of makeup and tamed her beautiful curly locks. When a knock on the door finally came, Trudy thought she would literally sprout wings and fly. Trudy's father opened the door and welcomed Paul inside. His aunt and her fiancé waited in the car. Trudy went to the top of the stairs and listened as her father instructed Paul.

"We would like to have Trudy home no later than ten-thirty."

"Yes sir," she heard her love answer.

"Also, I want you to know that Trudy is the most important thing in our lives. We would never want her hurt. We have raised her with a great deal of respect and we expect you to treat her the same way."

"Absolutely sir," Paul answered.

"I believe you are a fine young man, and that is the only reason we are allowing Trudy to go out with you tonight. Please prove to us that we are correct."

"I will sir, I promise."

Trudy rushed down the stairs trying to save Paul from any further discomfort. As soon as he saw her, he lit up.

"You look beautiful Trudy," he grinned.

Trudy smiled back, then Paul opened the door for her. Trudy looked back at her father and her mother, who had entered the foyer from the kitchen.

"I'll see you at ten-thirty," she gleefully smiled. Her mother returned the smile while her father remained stoic.

The two walked to the car and Paul opened the back door for her. Trudy got in and Miss Danton introduced her to her betrothed.

"Trudy, this is my fiancé, Mack Fields."

Trudy and Mack exchanged pleasantries before Trudy settled into the back seat next to Paul.

Neither Trudy, nor Paul, took their eyes off each other on the ride to Maiden. Miss Danton tried to make small talk with them, but they were so caught up in their own conversation that they failed to hear her. She smiled to herself, remembering when she and Mack were the same way.

The group stopped for dinner at the Silver Spoon, a small and intimate restaurant, before making their way to The Majestic to see *Kings Row* staring Ronald Regan, Ann Sheridan, and Robert Cummings.

Again Trudy and Paul buried their heads together as if they were Siamese Twins. They whispered throughout the movie in hushed and flirtatious tones. Miss Danton and Mack had to shush them a couple of times. The duo would sit silently for only a moment before commencing their banter again.

Paul took Trudy's hand in his and kissed it ever so gently. Trudy felt chills go up her spine. She smiled at him and he kissed it again. Luckily Miss Danton and Mack were engrossed in the film and did not see the exchange.

When the movie was over, the group walked down the street, Miss Danton peering into the windows of stores which had already closed. She pointed to outfits and told Mack that she liked them. Trudy and Paul laughed and giggled behind them.

"My mother and father asked you to come to Sunday dinner. My father will pick you up while my mother and I prepare it. Can you come?" Trudy excitedly asked.

"I'll need to check with my folks, but if it is okay with them, I would love to," Paul answered.

Trudy sighed. Could she be any happier?

The ride home was a blur, the two never ceasing their conversation. Paul held Trudy's hand the entire way. When they pulled into Trudy's driveway and stopped, Paul told his aunt and future Uncle to wait while he walked Trudy to the door.

Trudy felt like her heart was going to beat out of her chest. This was the moment. Although they had an audience, Trudy wanted more than anything for Paul to kiss her. He escorted her up onto her porch and to the front door.

"I had a swell time. Did you?" he asked her.

"Oh I did!" she exclaimed. "I hope you can come for dinner Sunday. How will I know?" she asked.

"I'm sure my folks will allow me to call for this," he answered, while looking down at the hands he was still holding.

"I guess I better be going." He shuffled his feet, kicking at imaginary dirt, before looking Trudy in the eyes.

"I guess so," Trudy answered, returning Paul's gaze.

Paul leaned into Trudy and brushed her lips with his. Every cell in her body went on alert and even when he took a step back, Trudy forgot to breathe.

Paul smiled at her and Trudy, wide eyed and still in shock, tried to speak but nothing was forthcoming.

"Hopefully I will see you on Sunday," Paul said, while backing down the porch steps.

Trudy didn't answer. She couldn't. Her head was swept in a million different directions, still caught up in her very first kiss.

Paul waved his hand before turning to leave. Trudy stared after him. He turned and waved again when he reached the car.

The door behind her opened and the voice of her father finally snapped her back to reality.

"Have a good time?" he asked.

"Um hmm," was all Trudy could manage before she entered the house and glided up the stairs to her room, her feet never touching the ground.

CHAPTER SEVENTEEN

Trudy spent hours that night replaying the kiss over again in her head. She didn't know what time she finally fell asleep but she knew it was late when she awoke. The sun was casting a large glowing stripe over the center of her bed. She tossed the covers aside and sat up. Had the previous night been real? Did she really get her first kiss from the love of her life?

When she surmised it was real, she sighed and smiled to herself. She was more in love than any human had the capacity to be. She convinced herself that no one had ever felt love for another to the extent she had for Paul, not even her parents.

How could they? This was a magical love that was only possible between Trudy and Paul. This was a one-time event, so huge that God Himself could not recreate it a second time. A moment of sadness came over her, knowing that the rest of the world would never experience what she had.

Trudy heard the phone ringing in the kitchen. She sat lost in her own memories before she heard her mother call up the stairs to her.

"Trudy?" Elsa queried, "Paul is on the phone for you, are you awake?"

Trudy bounded from the bed, not even bothering to put on her robe or slippers. She ripped open her door and almost tripped herself trying to get down the stairs.

Elsa backed away as Trudy headed toward her, sensing that if she didn't, she would be run over.

"Hello?" Trudy breathlessly answered as she grabbed the phone.

"Hi!" she heard Paul say.

"Hi!" Trudy answered.

"I wanted to call and tell you that I can come for dinner tomorrow if the invitation still stands."

"Oh yes, of course it does!" Trudy almost yelled in her excitement. "My dad will come and get you right after church if that is okay."

"Actually, my folks said I could take their car. I got my license about four months ago," Paul told her.

"Oh, okay," Trudy hadn't even considered that Paul could drive, because even though she was old enough to have her license too, she just didn't see the point.

"I can't stay on long," Paul interrupted her thought, "but I wanted to tell you again how much I enjoyed last night. I hope it won't be long before we can do it again. Maybe next time we can just go by ourselves," he added.

"I would like that so much," Trudy hesitantly answered, while wondering if her parents would allow it. Surely after really getting to know Paul at Sunday's dinner, they would.

"What time should I be there?" Paul again interrupted Trudy's thoughts.

"One," she answered.

"Swell," Paul replied. "I'll see you then. Goodbye Trudy,"

"Goodbye Paul," she sighed.

Trudy hung up the phone and relayed the information to her mother before running back up to her room to get her robe and slippers. She then returned to the kitchen as her mother fried her an egg and put it and some toast in front of her.

"Did you enjoy your date?" Elsa tried to act nonchalant about the ordeal, although she wanted more than anything for Trudy to share the details of her first date.

Elsa and Knute had never had a "first date." While they had gone on dates, it was no different than any other day because they had always done everything together. In fact, thay had never spent a day apart from each other until Knute worked the rigs and they were already married.

Elsa turned to look at her daughter, who was dreamily staring at her plate, but not eating her breakfast. She sat down across the table from Trudy.

"Did you have a nice time?" Elsa tried again.

Trudy released the gaze from her plate and turned it to her mother.

"Mother," you have no idea!" she gushed. "We had so much fun!"

She got up from her chair and sat in the one right next to Elsa, leaning in close to her. "We ate at the Silver Spoon and then went to The Majestic. We talked all night – even during the movie!" she giggled. "Mom, Paul is so nice. He's such a gentleman. He is perfect in every way."

Elsa watched her daughter's face morph into complete bliss as she talked about Paul.

"How was the movie?" Elsa questioned.

Trudy sat in silence for a moment thinking about her mother's question.

"Um, I don't really know," she finally confessed. "Paul was telling me all about his plans to play major league baseball after high school. I didn't really watch it because I wanted to talk to Paul!" She laughed.

Elsa had never seen Trudy this happy – not even before she had started school and spent hours frolicking through the fields with Knute, her grandparents, and Elsa. Trudy's face actually appeared to be lit from within.

"So Paul wants to continue to play baseball?" Elsa didn't want the moment of sharing to end, and hoped her daughter would let more of her feelings feed her mother's curiosity.

"Yes," Trudy obliged. "He said he might have to go to the minor leagues first, but he hopes he is good enough to just go to the majors." Trudy didn't stop for a breath. "His folks would like him to go on to college first and play ball there. They think he could go anywhere he wanted to but he wants to concentrate all his efforts on the game and not school."

She finally paused and breathed. "He also said he has thought about going into the Army first to help out with the war effort, but his dad thinks the war will be over before he gets out of school."

Elsa sat greedily absorbing every word from her child's mouth. She had learned more about Paul in the past few minutes than she had learned about him in the past several weeks.

"I hope he gets to play in the majors," Trudy continued to spill. "Wouldn't it be so neat to know a famous baseball player?" she asked her mother without waiting for an answer. "And I would be his girlfriend or even his wife." She grinned from ear to ear, as her eyes twinkled with the fantasy she was creating. "We could travel all over the United States together." Trudy sighed, not realizing she was releasing her most intimate desires to her mother.

"Wouldn't that be fabulous Mother? I would get to see the whole country and maybe if I decided to act, I could plan my performances around where Paul would play. It's perfect!"

Elsa began to get a little pang in her stomach. It was easy to see that her daughter was head over heels in love, and although she and Knute had the fairy tale love story, she knew

145

theirs was rare. She didn't want to see Trudy get hurt. She couldn't bear it.

"Trudy," Elsa interjected, "you are only finishing your sophomore year. There are still two years of school left for you and Paul. A lot can happen in that time. Don't you think it is too early for you to be making plans like this?"

Elsa immediately saw the look of betrayal on Trudy's face and regretted that she had voiced her concern.

"You don't understand, Mother. Of course you couldn't possibly because no one has what Paul and I have." She glared at the woman next to her. "We are meant to be together, so it doesn't matter that we still have two years of school. We are going to be together forever. You and Daddy have been together your whole lives. Just because I didn't meet Paul until now, doesn't mean that we aren't supposed to be together."

Trudy stood up from her chair and turned to leave the kitchen.

"Don't you want breakfast?" Elsa half pleaded, realizing that she had just shut down the fountain of information she so desperately wanted to drown in. She sighed, completely regretting her part in that.

"I'm not hungry," Trudy flatly stated. "I'm going upstairs to get dressed."

Elsa remained seated, trying to digest the enormous ramifications of what Trudy had just revealed.

She didn't know where to begin.

After church, Trudy rushed around frantically making sure the dinner table was perfect, her hair was perfect, the house was perfect, and her dress was perfect. She ran in and out of the kitchen to check on her mother's progress with dinner. She took a tea towel into the dining room and polished the silver and the glasses repeatedly. Although Trudy walked into the parlor several times to check the time on the grandfather clock, her father sat reading the Sunday paper, ignoring his daughter's antsiness.

At five minutes before one, Trudy ran upstairs to check her dress and hair one more time. Then she ran back down into the kitchen to make sure her mother was prepared.

"How much longer will the roast be?" she whined.

"Honey, calm down," Elsa replied. "It will be ready on time. Don't you want to have a few minutes to visit before we eat?"

Trudy hadn't thought about that, but it was the proper thing to do. She calmed down a little. At exactly one, a dark blue sedan rolled up the driveway. Trudy stood at the window watching her true love exit the car with a small bouquet of flowers in his hand. Paul strode to the porch and knocked on the wooden door. Trudy started to rush to the door. Her father stopped her.

"No you don't." He walked around her. "That is my job."

Knute opened the door to reveal his daughter's suitor.

"Hello Mr. Dahl," Paul extended his hand. "Thank you very much for inviting me to dinner."

"Hello Paul," Knute answered, while extending his own hand. "Please come in. We are happy to have you. Mrs. Dahl and I are looking forward to getting to know you better."

Paul entered the foyer before seeing Trudy standing at the entrance of the dining room. He smiled at her, and she back at him.

"Hi Trudy," he said, handing her the flowers. "These are for you and your mother."

"How pretty!" Trudy exclaimed. "I'll show her."

"Paul, why don't you come into the parlor with me. Maybe we can catch up on a little baseball." Knute turned to motion Paul into the room.

"I would like that, Sir."

Trudy took the flowers into the kitchen as the men made themselves comfortable in the parlor.

"Look, Mother," she said coolly, as if Paul had just proven how devoted he was to her. "Paul brought us flowers."

Elsa turned from the stove. "Well wasn't that so sweet of him?" she smiled at her daughter. "Why don't you put them in a vase and we will put them in the center of the table."

Trudy did as her mother suggested.

It wasn't long before dinner was done and Trudy and Elsa piled the table with food. Knute and Paul appeared in the doorway to marvel at the feast before them.

"Paul, you may sit here." Knute pointed to a side chair opposite of Trudy. Both Knute and Elsa took their seats at the table's ends, before Knute asked everyone to bow their heads for grace.

Knute began to pray, asking God to bless the food before them. Trudy snuck a peek at Paul, who was in turn, peeking at her. They both smiled.

"Amen," Knute declared, startling the two before they raised their heads, as if they too had been in prayer.

The group passed around the roast, potatoes, green beans, biscuits, and carrots. Both Paul and Knute's plates were piled high while Trudy and Elsa's contained only a fraction of what the men had acquired.

"Paul tells me that he thinks Ashton has a good chance of winning state this year, Dear," Knute nodded to Elsa.

"Isn't that wonderful?" she asked.

"How is your arm holding up?" Knute asked his guest.

"It's doing everything it should," Paul nodded. "I feel really fortunate that I've never had an injury. I guess all that hay stacking and hauling has been good for me after all," he chuckled.

"Where I grew up, we did a lot of corn harvesting and shucking," Knute interjected. "It was the best way to keep in shape for football."

Knute and Paul both immersed themselves in conversation about the sports they played. Trudy watched every interaction between the two as if she were observing a complex and intense science project. Elsa in turn, watched Trudy, while the familiar pang in her stomach made itself known.

Dinner finished, the men again retreated to the parlor while Elsa and Trudy cleared and washed the dishes. Finally, Trudy returned to Paul, bringing with her large slices of apple pie for him and her father. Elsa followed with two more pieces for Trudy and herself. The foursome sat in the parlor and ate their dessert, while Knute continued to ask Paul questions about his team and their season.

"Honey, we should let the kids talk a little, don't you think?" Elsa finally broke in. Trudy smiled her thanks to her mother.

"Oh, sorry," Knute apologized to Paul. "I just love the game. I can get carried away sometimes."

"Oh no, don't apologize. I could talk baseball all day," Paul responded. "It's nice to be able to talk to someone who loves it

151

as much as I do. My dad loves the game too, but he has a lot of other things he has to take care of, so we don't get to talk about it much." Paul seemed genuinely appreciative for the time he had gotten to spend with Knute.

"Help me in the kitchen," Elsa commanded Knute, as she ushered him out of the room, leaving the two teenagers alone.

Paul turned to Trudy. He took her hand in his and sat in silence for a moment before speaking.

"Trudy," he looked into her eyes, "I know I haven't known you but a couple of months but I feel like we have known each other our whole lives."

Trudy sucked in her breath. Was this the moment she has dreamed of since first meeting Paul? Was he going to declare that he loved her as much as she loved him? She almost felt like she was going to faint.

"Trudy, I was wondering if you would go steady with me?" Paul finally managed.

Trudy didn't quite comprehend his question at first. She had been waiting for him to declare his love and her brain stumbled to make sense of his words. Steady? Hadn't they already been going steady? She certainly hadn't dated anyone else. Had he?

Paul saw the confusion in Trudy's face and mistook it.

"I'm sorry. It was too soon for me to ask you that wasn't it? Just forget it," he stumbled, embarrassed that she didn't feel the same way he did.

Finally processing the events, Trudy jumped up. "Oh no, no Paul," she gasped. "It's not too soon. I'm the one who is sorry. I just didn't understand what you were asking. I guess I thought we were already going steady because I haven't been seeing anyone else. Have you?" Trudy got a horrified look on her face, almost dreading his answer.

"Oh no, Trudy. I don't – I haven't wanted to date anyone else since I met you. You are the only girl I want to see," he reassured her.

Trudy sat back down on the couch and sighed, her knees shook with the knowledge that her relationship with Paul might have just ended. Her heart also skipped with the knowledge that he had been faithful to only her. When she regained her composure, she turned to him.

"I would love to go steady with you Paul," she smiled. He smiled back, and lovingly took her hand in his again.

"Great then, it's settled. We are going steady."

Elsa and Knute watched from the kitchen, trying to keep out of sight of the two.

"And to think we were worried she would never date," Elsa whispered to Knute.

"Well, I guess if she is going to have a boyfriend, he's the one she should have," Knute replied.

Elsa squeezed Knute's hand before patting it. She knew it was much harder on a father to watch a daughter fall in love, than it was a mother. She squeezed his hand again.

CHAPTER EIGHTEEN

T he next two years of Trudy's life flew as if time has collapsed in on itself. She continued acting and starring in all of the school plays. She won the state competition in dramatic prose, humorous duet, and group performance, both her junior and senior years. The little town of Konawa was abuzz with talk of her leaving and becoming a Hollywood starlet.

Paul's life had been much the same. Not only did Ashton indeed take the state baseball title at the end of his sophomore year, but also his junior year. Scouts had been coming from all over the country to the last half of season games, and they loved what they saw.

Trudy and Paul spent every moment that they could together. They continued writing letters, but not as much as before because Paul was allowed to take the family car to Konawa on the weekends and see Trudy. Trudy and her family had been invited to Paul's home at Thanksgiving and the favor was returned by Trudy's parents at Christmas. The families bonded, much like Knute's and Elsa's had, back before the turn of the century.

Miss Danton, who was now Mrs. Fields, still asked Trudy to attend out of town games with her because Mack had to work and she very much enjoyed the company. In fact, she was sure that someday, she and Trudy would be related through marriage. She knew the kids were only seniors in high school, but a lot of the time, her students got married immediately following graduation.

Although Paul had still not been formally asked to join either a major league or minor league team, his chances looked promising. His senior season would be what decided it all.

The war still had not ended as his father had predicted. But having the scouts watch him play made him lean more toward baseball than enlisting. However Paul understood there was still a chance that he could be drafted by the military. If he was, he was more than willing to go. He figured that he could still play when he came home. Trudy wouldn't speak of it with him. It was just too scary and painful of a proposition for her to bear, knowing that not only would he have to leave her for an extended amount of time, but that he could be leaving her for good.

The lovebirds had a lot of time to spend together during the fall, since the season hadn't started. On Friday nights they would go into Konawa and have a burger at the Eater Upper. Other kids from both schools would also be there, and although Paul was friendly and might visit with his buddies a short while, his attention mostly remained focused on Trudy. Trudy actually didn't mind Paul's friends stopping at their table to chat. She especially liked his friend Wendy Williams, who dated Paul's best friend, and the catcher on the baseball team, Jeff Tyler. They were friendly and she felt more comfortable with them than she ever had her own classmates. In fact, it was the first time she actually felt like part of a group. Even the drama club hadn't done that for her, because of all the jealousy.

In January, Paul warned Trudy that their time was about to be limited.

"We start indoor training next week. That means that I will be staying after school late, and by the time I get home to get chores done, eat dinner, and do my homework, there won't be any time left."

Trudy scowled, even though she had been through the same thing before their junior year. She eased her discomfort by telling herself that although she would miss him dearly, at least they could still write letters and see each other on the weekends.

"I'm excited about this season," Paul told her. "Just think, I might be picked up to play professionally," he beamed.

Each time Paul would speak of his future, Trudy waited for him to mention his plans for her, but he didn't. She tried broaching the subject a time or two, but Paul never caught on to what she wanted – a commitment that he wouldn't leave her behind.

"I'm not sure what I'm going to do after I graduate," she would say aloud. Paul usually acted as if he hadn't even heard her, instead planning his entry into the Big Game.

"I wonder what it is like to play in front of so many people?" he would reply.

Trudy answered with "I can't wait to see you play," hoping he would say "You will see me play all my games Honey, because you will be my wife."

She was disappointed that he never did.

Trudy told herself that as soon as the season was over and Paul was offered a position, he would realize that he couldn't leave her. It would be then that he would ask her to marry him. It never dawned on her that it could be any different. She was sure there was no other alternative because Paul couldn't live without her any more than she could live without him.

The season began and Paul was even better on the mound than his three previous seasons as the leader of his state championship team. He had developed an unshakeable confidence. It was as if he knew exactly where each batter's weak spot was, and he would sail his pitches to match that exact area.

The first half of the season he pitched seven no-hitters in a row. More and more scouts were making stops in the little rural towns of Oklahoma where Paul and the Ashton Chieftains played.

One Friday evening in April, Paul and Trudy, as they usually did, went into Konawa to have a burger. Trudy had continued hinting to Paul about their future together, but it was as if he was completely oblivious. She almost thought that maybe Paul didn't even think of it – or at the very least, not nearly as much as she did.

"Paul," she finally posed, "when you leave Ashton, what do you want me to do?"

Paul looked at her, confused. "What do you mean?"

"Well," she cocked her head to one side, "do you plan on me staying here or do you want me to go with you?"

Paul raised his eyebrows and nervously cleared his throat. "I don't think I understand what you are asking," he finally managed.

Trudy began to get tense. Why was Paul acting this way? He must have given it thought at some point. They had been together over two years, and they were madly in love. It only made sense that they would take the next step.

"I mean, are you going to take me with you when you go? Are we going to get married?"

Paul, who had been sipping a cola, began choking. Soda, splattered all over the table and even on Trudy's dress. Trudy got up and hit him on the back, trying to help him get his breath. When he finally cleared his throat and regained his composure, he sat silently for a long time. The longer he sat, the more upset Trudy became.

"Surely you have thought about this," she declared. "I mean, do you just expect me to sit here in Konawa and wait for you until you are done playing ball?"

Paul remained silent.

"Paul?" Trudy scrunched her face trying to see into his mind. "Paul?" she asked again.

It seemed like forever to Trudy before he finally answered.

"Trudy, I haven't really thought about it and for that I'm sorry. I guess I should have, but I've been so caught up in just hoping I get picked up that I didn't. Also, there is no guarantee that I will be going anywhere. Anything can happen between now and then. I may get hurt. The scouts may not like what they see, and even if they do, they may not have a place for me." He reached for her hand.

"To be honest, I guess a part of me thinks it won't happen. Don't get me wrong, I want it to, but a part of me is scared that it won't. Part of me is scared that I will have to go to war. Part of me thinks maybe I will go to college and if so, that you will go too."

Trudy sighed. Everything he had told her made sense. She could see the uncertainty, and even some fear in his eyes.

"Oh Paul," she soothed, "please don't worry. I know everything is going to work out. The scouts would be crazy not to want you. I know you are going to play baseball. I just know it!"

Paul smiled at her. "I hope you are right and just in case you are, I'm going to think about what we have talked about. I promise."

Trudy smiled and laughed. She was so relieved that she had finally had the talk with him. Now she knew they were on the same page and that page said "Happily ever after!"

CHAPTER NINETEEN

The following Tuesday, Ashton again played Konawa. Trudy met her father and mother at the field. They sat next to Paul's parents and his aunt.

Ashton took the field first. Paul put a curve over the plate on the first pitch and Konawa senior, Roger Harris, smacked it long, between right and center field. He rounded first, then second, and at the motioning of his coach, slid into third where he was safe.

Paul looked a little shocked. He had played against Roger since they were freshmen. He knew his weak spot was low and tight. He was sure that was where he had delivered the ball.

Paul looked at his best friend and catcher. Jeff mouthed to him to shake it off. Paul took a deep breath and watched as number 12 came to the plate. He couldn't remember the batter's name although he had played against him for years. He also couldn't remember his weak spot. Paul looked at Jeff again. He motioned for a fast ball. Paul having no idea if it was the right thing to do, had no choice but to throw it.

The bat cracked and the ball sailed in between shortstop and second. Both tried to dive to get it, but missed. Jeff headed home and number 12 ran onto first. The center threw to Paul who watched the runner until he was sure he wasn't moving on.

Paul had not allowed two straight hits at all the entire season. He was a little unnerved.

"It's okay boy," Hollis Somerton yelled to his son. "You got this next one. Strike 'em out!"

Paul glanced at his Dad and nodded. He watched Jim Spencer step into the batter's box. Spencer played football too, and was often named MVP of their games. Paul remembered that Jim had trouble with Paul's splitter. Jeff must have remembered it too because that is what he motioned for Paul to throw. Paul nodded his agreement to the catcher and let the splitter sail from his hands.

"Strike!" the umpire yelled.

"Good job Son," Paul heard his father yell.

"Keep it up," his coach added.

Jeff again called for a splitter. Paul agreed and released the ball.

Jim connected and sent it grounded and whooshing by Paul's feet. It was already past him before he even saw it. The first baseman leapt to retrieve it behind the run line. Number 12 was already landing on second before he got it. He turned just in time to see Spencer hit the base, free and clear.

Paul was dumbfounded. He hadn't let a grounder past him since he was a kid. What was going on? He felt fine. He thought his pitches were right where they were supposed to be. How could those players be hitting like they were batting against a third grader?

"Time," Paul heard his coach yell before he came to the mound.

"What's going on Son?" he asked.

"I don't know." Paul shook his head. "Everything feels right. What are you seeing?"

"Honestly?" his coached looked him in the eye as if asking if he really wanted to the brutal truth.

"Yeah," Paul answered.

"You're slow. You're more than slow. Your pitches are coming in like a damn turtle. Where's your heat?"

Paul's eyes widened. He hadn't seen that or felt it. He thought each pitch was delivered with the same speed he had always been known for.

"Are you sure Coach? I mean, I'm telling you, everything feels exactly right to me."

"I'm sure. Ask Jeff," he said, pointing to the catcher and telling him to come to the mound.

"Does Somerton look slow to you?" he asked the boy.

Jeff looked at his cleats, as if he didn't want to be the bearer of bad news. "Yeah," he finally managed. "They're slow Paul."

Paul shook his head in disbelief. He kicked the dirt a moment before looking at his coach.

"Okay, if you say I'm slow, then I'm slow. I'll put some more heat on it."

"Make sure you do," the coach replied. "Got a scout here." He motioned to the top left side of the bleachers.

The coach and Jeff walked back to their places. Paul sighed, still unable to grasp that his pitches were slow. It didn't make sense. Why wasn't he feeling it?

Finally he took the mound again and readied himself for Rick Cody, Konawa's catcher, who was known as a great cleanup hitter. Jeff motioned for another curve ball and Paul acknowledged him.

"Put some heat on it," he told himself. *"Put. Some. Heat. On. It."*

He wound up and let the ball fly. It wasn't a curve. It wasn't a fastball. It wasn't a cutter or any other kind of pitch Paul was familiar with. What it did end up being was a homerun. Just like that, Konawa led four to zero.

Paul finally managed two strikeouts after letting two more players on base. Chuck Bayless, Konawa's first baseman, stepped up to the plate. Paul knew he had to stop the bleeding and get Chuck out. Bayless was a powerhouse. He usually never hit less than a double, but mostly opted for triples and homeruns. Paul began to sweat.

Jeff called for a screwball. Paul shook his head no. A screwball was the hardest pitch for Paul. He usually nailed it, but he had to have just the precise amount of speed and spin to get it to drop at the right time. On any other day, it would have been no big deal. But Paul had lost his confidence and this pitch was too important. He couldn't take a chance.

His friend called for it a second time, but again, Paul refused. Finally his catcher signaled for a cutter. Paul nodded, readied himself and let it go.

Bayless nailed it on the sweet spot and the ball sailed over the third baseman with so much power it looked like it was headed for the cosmos. The left fielder took off running as fast as he could toward the fence. He backed all the way up to it before realizing that the ball was going, going, gone. He threw his glove to the ground.

Paul hit his knees. He had never experienced anything like this. It was nothing short of humiliating, and it was heartbreaking, because he knew he had let down his entire team. When it really counted, he had not been there for them.

One more batter got to second before Paul managed to strike out the third player. There was no jubilation though. The team slowly returned to the dugout, dazed and confused.

The rest of the game wasn't much better than the first inning. Ashton managed to score six of their own runs, but Konawa dominated them with thirteen of their own. It was the worst game Paul had ever played and he was sickened.

As Trudy, Knute, Elsa, and Paul's parents stood in awkward silence while waiting for him after the game, Paul finally ambled over to the group, head low. He didn't make eye contact with any of them, including Trudy.

"Everyone has a bad game," Hollis Somerton consoled his son. "It's a real miracle that you haven't had one before now."

"It's only one game," Knute chimed in. "You got the rest of the season to whip up on these teams."

"It's okay Paul, we are all still really proud of you," Trudy ducked her head below his, trying to get him to look at her.

"I appreciate it," Paul finally answered. "I've got to get on the bus."

He took Trudy's hand and squeezed it before he turned to go.

Thursday's game with Wheeler went much the way Tuesday's had gone. Paul's coach called time in the third inning and approached his pitcher.

"Son, what is going on with you? You are not in this ballgame and if you don't get back in, I've got no choice but to pull you."

Paul looked shocked. "Coach, no. I can do this," he pleaded. "I don't know what's happening. Just give me the rest of the inning. If I'm not up to speed, then pull me."

"Alright, ya got 'til the rest of the inning. Get it done." The coach spit some tobacco juice onto the diamond before he returned to the dugout.

After the inning, and four more runs, the coach pulled Paul.

He was more than rattled. He had never felt so bad in his life. It was as if someone had told him he had cancer and only a couple of weeks left to live. In fact, he didn't want to live if he couldn't play ball.

He had to figure out what was going on and soon.

CHAPTER TWENTY

Friday evening Paul went to Trudy's house. They decided to have dinner and visit with her parents instead of going out. Paul was exceptionally quite during the meal although Knute tried on several occasions to engage him. Finally Elsa gave Knute a look which told him to let Paul be.

When the meal was finished, Elsa took the lead. "Trudy, why don't you and Paul go ahead into the parlor? Dad and I will clean the dishes. I'm sure you all will want to talk about plans for the Senior Class Ball."

Trudy thanked her mother and led Paul away.

"I've been meaning to talk to you about the ball. I'm glad Mother brought it up," she told him.

Paul didn't answer. Trudy could see his mind was elsewhere.

"Do you want to talk about anything Paul?" she asked.

"No, I'm sorry, I didn't mean to ignore you. I'm just a little preoccupied tonight."

"I know." Trudy, brushed some hair from his eyes. "Please tell me if I can help in any way. I want to help you know, because we are a team."

Paul took a deep breath. "No, it's okay. I will figure things out," he replied. "Let's get back to that ball. Tell me about it."

Trudy told Paul about the ball that would be held in two weeks, before the end of school.

"It's only seniors and their dates. We will have dinner and then a lot of dancing. I would really like it if you went with me. You will have to wear a suit. Mother said I can buy an evening dress. Will you go?"

"Of course I will," Paul answered. "And I already know you will be the most beautiful girl there."

Trudy smiled, but she saw in Paul's eyes he was not as excited as she was. Hopefully he would begin pitching better and get back to his old self again. When that happened, she knew they would have the night of their lives.

"Okay, well pick me up at six-thirty. Dinner will be at seven, followed by the ball!" She merrily clapped her hands together before kissing Paul on the cheek. "We are going to have so much fun!"

The following day, Trudy and her mother went into Maiden to the Smart Shoppe to find an evening gown for Trudy. Trudy tried on several, before settling on aquamarine chiffon with dainty iridescent sequins. It made her eyes shine like the sky.

After a light lunch at Delia's Tea Room, they made their way to the Shoe Chalet'. Trudy picked out a pair of satin pumps which she could would have dyed to match her dress. The store not only could dye them, but they told her they could add little marabou poofs to the toes. Trudy was ecstatic, thinking they would be the prettiest shoes anyone had ever seen.

"Oh Mother," Trudy exclaimed as they left the store, "I'm going to have the prettiest outfit at the ball! I can't wait to go. Paul and I are going to have the best time! I can't wait to dance with him," she added. "He says he is pretty good and that makes me really happy that you made me take dance lessons."

Elsa smiled at her beautiful daughter. She too, couldn't wait for the evening when she would see the once shy, little blonde girl, turn into an elegant and sophisticated young woman. She was almost as excited as Trudy.

The two ladies put their packages in the car and returned home to show Knute what they had found. They both ran into the house and cornered him in the parlor as he sat reading the evening paper.

"Look at my dress, Daddy!" Trudy scrambled to remove it from the large box where it was housed. She held it up to herself and swung her hips to show off how it flowed.

"Isn't it divine?" she squealed.

Knute tried to sound enthusiastic. "It is my dear. It is!"

Elsa smiled at him. "Our daughter is going to be the most beautiful girl at the ball." She winked at Knute.

Trudy smiled at her mother.

"That she is," Knute agreed. "And speaking of the ball," he said, laying his paper aside, "I thought that maybe you and Paul might like to take the Cadillac?"

"Oh yes!" Trudy replied. "I can't wait to tell Paul. He loves your car Daddy."

"He should," Knute laughed. "Getting that took a small miracle considering they had to stop making cars and start making tanks for the war. I'm lucky to have it."

The three remained in the parlor talking about the upcoming ball. Knute finally changed the subject to Paul's problems on the mound.

"Has Paul told you if anything is bothering him?" Knute asked Trudy. "I felt bad that he had such a poor showing in front of that scout. Hollis said he really hasn't seen any improvement since."

"No Daddy, I've asked him but he doesn't really answer. He seems very preoccupied but I don't know if it's because he is playing bad, or if he is playing bad because he is preoccupied."

"Well let's hope he snaps out of it soon. There's a lot riding on the way he plays these next few weeks."

Trudy sighed. "I know."

As she lay in bed that night, she wondered if it might be such a bad thing if Paul didn't get picked up by a team.

"Maybe we can go to college together. Maybe we can go ahead and get married," she surmised. She began to mentally create a life with Paul without baseball being a part of it.

"*I might be able to become an actress and Paul could move with me to Hollywood,*" she dreamed. "*We would love it in California. I could become as famous as Greta Garbo. Paul will look so handsome escorting me to the Academy Awards.*"

Trudy fell asleep with stars in her eyes – the biggest one, being herself.

CHAPTER TWENTY-ONE

P aul had left Trudy's that previous night, not really remembering much of their conversation. He knew he had committed to taking her to her Senior Class Ball. She had said something about him needing a suit. He would have to ask his mother to help him get one. He could also wear it to graduation. After he milked Miss Molly, he headed to slop the pigs. His head would not stop swimming.

"Why have I been pitching so poorly? Why can't I get it right? It doesn't make sense."

Lost in his thoughts, he failed to hear his father behind him.

"Paul!" he finally heard Hollis yell, before turning around to see him pointing at the slop bucket.

"You just gonna stand there all day with an empty bucket? Hogs won't be putting on any weight if you aren't gonna feed 'em."

Paul hadn't realized that, although he had been "slopping" the animals, he hadn't put anything in the bucket to slop them with.

"Oh, golly Dad, I don't know what is wrong with me." He turned to go back to the porch to get the leftovers and scraps from their meals.

"Son, just what is wrong with you?" His father caught his arm before he left. "You can talk to me you know. I'll help you anyway I can."

Paul turned to face his father. "I don't know Dad. I mean, when I'm on the mound, everything feels normal. I even see the pitches as normal, but Coach and Jeff both say I'm slow. And you've seen for yourself that I'm nowhere near my mark."

"Let's think about this a moment. When did your slump come on?" his father questioned.

"The Konawa game was the first time. But it hasn't stopped in over two weeks now. I doubt Coach is going to let me play at all anymore."

"Did anything unusual happen that day at school?"

"No sir, nothing that I can remember."

"What about in the days before? Did something happen to upset you? Did someone say something that bothered you?"

Paul thought about the Monday before the game and couldn't think of anything out of the ordinary. He then went back to Sunday and realized he was a little on edge that day. In fact, he had forgotten to lock up the chicken coop that night and a coyote had gotten a couple of their fowl.

"You remember when I forgot to lock up the chickens?" he asked Hollis.

"Yeah, is that what's upsetting you? Because I know I was mad at you because we lost some good laying hens, but heck Son, what's done is done. Don't let it get you down any longer."

"No dad, I don't think I'm down about the chickens, but I think I forgot to lock them up because I wasn't thinking straight, just like today."

"Well do you know why?" his father queried.

Paul thought some more. Nothing had happened Sunday to upset him, but he did know his feelings weren't sitting right. He thought back to Saturday and remembered feeling a little uneasy then too. In fact when Trudy wanted him to come to Konawa to go to the picture show, he told her he wasn't feeling well and he stayed home. That was definitely unusual for him. He would do almost anything to get to spend time with her.

"Have you figured it out?" his dad interrupted his quest.

"I was feeling kind of bad on that Saturday too, but I can't put my finger on why."

Paul continued thinking back to that weekend. Friday he had gone out with Trudy to get burgers at the Eater Upper. They had talked about him going to the majors and she had asked him what she was supposed to do. With that thought, Paul's stomach lurched.

"Trudy wants to get married," Paul said. He turned to look at his dad. "She asked me what she was supposed to do if I went to the big leagues. She asked if I was going to take her with me when I went. She asked if we were going to get married." Paul's eyes revealed his panic to his father.

Hollis cleared his throat. "Well Son, that's a pretty big thing, don't you think? What did you tell her?"

"I didn't really. I told her I was sorry that I hadn't included her in my plans and I told her that I would make sure and think about things – about our future."

"Have you?" Hollis questioned. "Have you thought about a future with her?

"No, not really," Paul admitted. "I thought I would have plenty of time after the season. I thought I should at least wait to see if I got an offer – to see if I was even leaving."

"Son, it sounds like you have a lot of pressure on you, and you may not realize it's there, but it is. Even though you haven't consciously given it much thought, it sounds like it is all your subconscious is able to think about. It's why you're not really in the game."

Paul couldn't believe it. Was that conversation really the reason he wasn't able to pitch? It made some sense. He had been taken off guard when Trudy broached the subject. He had even been a little taken aback. He was not ready to get married. He loved Trudy, but there were still so many things he wanted to experience before settling down and becoming a family man. He was sure that someday he would want to marry Trudy if she were still single when he was ready to give up baseball and start a family. But, he would never ask her to wait for him. He would never be that selfish.

"What am I going to do Dad?" Paul's eyes pleaded for an answer.

"You have to decide what is most important to you, Son. Do you want to play ball? Because if you do, you can't let anything or anyone get in the way. One hundred percent of your focus has to be on the game at all times. If you feel like you've had enough and you are ready to do something else, then Trudy may be the answer," he scratched his head. "We love her and we love her family. We would support you making a life with her."

"I do love her, but I'm not ready to give up ball. It's what I want to do more than anything. I would be thrilled if Trudy and I someday married, but I'm not ready yet. I have to go see if I can make it in the majors. I would never forgive myself if I didn't at least try," he whispered, as if saying it aloud would cause Trudy to hear.

"You have your answer then, Son."

"I don't know how to tell her, Dad. It will crush her. She has never even dated anyone else. She has her heart set on us being together. How can I possibly tell her I'm choosing baseball over her?"

"I know you are going to do the right thing." Hollis put his hand on the boy's shoulder. "This is one of those times when being a man is tough. But to be a man, you have to do the right thing, even when it's hard."

Paul nodded his understanding, but he still didn't know how he was going to go through with breaking Trudy's heart.

CHAPTER TWENTY-TWO

A week went by, with Trudy floating through the halls, dreaming of the day Paul would pop the question. She really wanted to talk with him about it more but with end of the year activities and Paul's games, the two had not been able to see each other. It was Friday and Trudy hoped Paul would come over that night, so that they could visit some more about their future nuptials, but also, the following week's dance.

Although she wanted more than anything to show Paul her dress, she agreed with herself that she wouldn't, because she wanted him to be surprised. She imagined his face when he watched her descend the stairs in her perfect gown, with perfect hair, and perfect shoes. He was going to have his socks blown off.

She asked her mother if she could call Paul to see what plans they might make together. Elsa agreed.

"Hello Mrs. Somerton," Trudy said, as Paul's mother answered the phone. "This is Trudy. How are you?"

"Well hello to you Trudy," Imogene Somerton seemed happy to hear from her. "I'm just wonderful. How are your mom and dad? I hope we can all get together again soon."

"I know they would like that," Trudy replied. "I hope we can too. By any chance is Paul available?"

"No Honey, I'm sorry. He's in the back-forty clearing some fallen trees with his dad. Is there anything I can help you with?" Imogene asked sweetly.

"No ma'am. I was just going to see if he was planning on coming over tonight. We haven't made any plans and I was just wondering," she sighed.

"Well, I'll tell you what. As soon as I see him, I'll have him call you."

"Thank you Mrs. Somerton. Please tell Mr. Somerton 'Hello' for me."

"I will Dear. Please tell your folks the same for me."

"I will. Goodbye."

"Goodbye."

Trudy hung up the phone. It was already five in the afternoon. Surely Paul wouldn't be much longer. She decided to take a hot bath and wash her hair, just in case he came.

"Trudy, dinner!" she heard her mother yell from downstairs.

"Dinner?" Trudy thought. *"We have dinner at six. Surely Paul is back from cutting trees by now. Why hasn't he called?"* she asked herself.

Trudy went downstairs and joined her parents for ham and beans. She walked in to hear her mother tell Knute how tired she was from picking up Trudy's new dyed shoes and shopping for some accessories for her daughter.

"Trudy's dance has almost worn me out," her mother laughed. "And by the way, I found a beautiful feather boa that will look stunning around your shoulders." Elsa beamed at her daughter.

"You did? Oh Mother, those are all the rage in Hollywood right now!" Trudy smiled broadly. "That is just perfect! After all, it's not every day that a girl in Southern Oklahoma gets to go to a ball."

"I'm sure glad of that," her mother replied, wiping fake perspiration from her brow.

The three continued to talk throughout dinner, discussing the ball and Trudy's upcoming graduation which would be held in just a few short weeks.

"You have so many choices. How exciting for you!" Knute smiled. "Have you decided what you are going to do? Have you decided which college you are going to attend?"

Trudy shifted in her seat. She wasn't ready to tell her parents about the conversation she had with Paul. She wanted to surprise them when he finally asked her to marry him, before they left together for the majors.

"I'm still not sure," she hesitantly answered. "I'm leaning more toward The University of Oklahoma than I am East Central Normal. I think they have a better drama program since East Central's is so new. But I seriously haven't ruled out going straight to Hollywood."

"Dear," her mother interjected, "Hollywood is always going to be there. There are more things you will learn in college that you are going to need throughout your life. I really hope you will at least give school a couple of years before leaving."

Knute nodded his agreement. "Your mother is right. It is better to be a well-educated actress than just an actress – in case things don't work out." He cut into a piece of ham.

"Oh Daddy, things are going to work out fine. Just you wait and see," Trudy assured him.

When the trio finished their meal, Trudy helped her mother clean up, while her father had coffee in the parlor.

They continued their discussion about Trudy's future, but Trudy was distracted, wondering why Paul had not called.

Maybe the job was a big one and he was still in the field. She knew if that was the case, he would be exhausted by the time he got home and wouldn't be coming over. She checked the clock in the parlor. It was six forty-five. Maybe he would call before seven-thirty and could at least come visit for an hour or two.

Elsa made some tea and the two joined Knute. Trudy watched the clock which slowly clicked away the minutes until it was eight. She accepted then that she wouldn't be seeing Paul that night.

"No matter," she placated herself, *"We will be seeing each other all the time in just a few weeks."* She smiled to herself,

thinking about the many plans she would need to make for her wedding.

Trudy knew she wanted something small and intimate, but still elegant. Maybe she would opt for an outdoor affair. If Paul was going to have his socks blown off after seeing her dressed for the ball, wait until he saw her in her wedding dress. He would positively melt.

Trudy told her parents she was going to her room to read, but what she did instead, was go through the latest issue of *Vogue* and *Movie Star Parade* to look at the newest fashion trends and try to decide what style bodice she might want for her wedding gown. There was a nice bridal shoppe in Maiden, but for her wedding, she thought she should go all the way to Oklahoma City to find a dress. Or better yet, she could even have it custom made. She was pretty good at drawing and she often passed the time in some of her boring classes sketching outfits.

"Wouldn't it be grand if I designed my own dress?" she sighed.

The idea stuck and she jumped from atop her bed to get a pencil and some paper from her desk. Why hadn't she thought of this before? Hopefully it wasn't too late to get a dress made.

Surely she and Paul would have to be married before the end of summer. She would need to get the design finished immediately.

Trudy worked until almost midnight sketching several versions of her ideal dress. She thought she had come up with almost the perfect design, but her eyes began to droop and she had to lay it aside.

"It's okay," she told herself. After all, she would have the entirety of Saturday to work on it.

She drifted off, dreamily telling herself that she wouldn't tell Paul about her perfect dress until he proposed. Wouldn't he be surprised at how talented his bride to be was? Trudy smiled to herself as her eyes grew ever heavier. She couldn't wait to be Mrs. Paul Somerton.

CHAPTER TWENTY-THREE

I mogene Somerton told her son that Trudy had called when he got home around five-thirty. He mumbled something about needing to clean up first. After dinner, his mother must have forgotten about the call, because she never mentioned it again.

Paul hadn't forgotten. He just wasn't prepared to talk to Trudy yet. There were so many things he needed to think through. Even though his father told him he had his answer, he wasn't sure he did. He couldn't just tell the girl he loved that he had decided baseball was more important than marrying her. Maybe it wasn't, and that was something he needed to figure out.

Paul didn't sleep the entire night. Instead he toyed with every possible scenario of how to make a relationship with Trudy work and still be able to pursue his life's calling.

He knew Trudy would be a wonderful wife. She was so attentive to him. She was incredibly supportive. She was more beautiful than any girl he had ever known. Most importantly, he was absolutely sure that, because of her kindness, she would make a wonderful mother someday. He came to realize that the problem wasn't with Trudy; the problem was with him.

Paul calculated that he wouldn't be able to devote the time to Trudy that she would need. He would be leaving her for long periods of time, especially during training camp. She would be lonely and unhappy. What if he was picked up somewhere where Trudy wouldn't be able to visit her parents? Or worse, what if she had no way to pursue her own dreams of being an actress? There were just too many uncertainties, and he could not ask anyone, much less Trudy, to sacrifice like that for him. And even if he could, the guilt alone would make it impossible for him to concentrate on the game.

The world of baseball was too competitive. There would always be someone waiting in line if he couldn't perform. He couldn't take that chance. He knew he had to give it everything he had – lock, stock, and barrel – because he could not spend the rest of his life wondering "What if?" He wasn't the type of person who could leave the game not knowing if he could have done better. He realized he had to leave everything on the field. It was the only way he knew how to be.

As he continued to search for ways that would prevent him from decimating Trudy, he thought that maybe he should promise to come back and marry her after he had played for a while. Then he concluded that he had no idea how long he planned to play. It was only normal that Trudy would ask, but he wouldn't be able to give her any sort of answer. He couldn't, because if he was as good as everyone said he was, he would not be able to walk away from the game when he was at his peak. Paul shook his head in frustration. It wasn't fair to Trudy to ask her to wait for what might be years.

A sinking feeling in his stomach was taking over. He wiped his sweaty brow with the back of his shirt sleeve then took a deep breath to try and calm his rapidly beating heart. He tried to console himself.

"If I fail. If I get don't make it, maybe Trudy won't be married yet. There's no doubt I will ask her then."

That worked for a moment to give him some relief but then reality set in. Trudy was too gorgeous and there would be more than plenty of suitors ready to marry her at a moment's notice. Thinking she would be around in a couple of years, was next to crazy.

"What if I skip the pros for now and go on to college and she goes with me there?" he asked himself. But he was answered with the fact that they would be in the exact same boat if he got picked up by the pros while there.

When Paul couldn't make marriage and baseball fit together, he actually considered giving up his dream of playing, in order to marry the girl he loved. The antsiness he felt before magnified itself by a hundred times.

If he didn't play ball, he would go into the service because he felt if he wasn't going to pursue his dream, it was his duty to serve his country. He shook his head again. Serving would mean leaving Trudy almost immediately. It also meant that he might make a widow of her. That was something he couldn't live with.

In an irrational moment, Paul even toyed with the idea of pushing her to go after her acting career in Hollywood. At least it would give her something to help her forget about him. After all, she loved acting almost as much as she loved him. It was *her* passion, as baseball was his. He surmised that she really did have a shot at it because she was so talented. He told himself that keeping her from it was selfish. Surely he could make her see that. Maybe he actually could convince her that she wanted an acting career more than she wanted to be with him. He told himself that she might even be relieved if he gave her his blessing.

It was only a few seconds before reality set in. Trudy had never mentioned that she wanted to go to Hollywood and wanted him to come with her. She had only ever talked of going with him. Trudy was willing to give up her dream for him. Encouraging her to forget him, would be a slap in the face.

The hours passed until the horizon was kissed with the morning sun. Paul was exhausted but he had a clear answer. At the end of it all, Paul only knew one thing, and that was that he loved Trudy deeply, but he was not going to be anyone's husband, especially hers, until he could give her one hundred and ten percent of himself. It was what had been modeled to him by his mother and father, and his own future children deserved the same. Marrying Trudy now would mean she might get fifty percent of him at best. That was not good enough for Trudy – not for his beautiful, smart and talented Trudy Dahl. He was almost ashamed of himself for even considering marrying her now, knowing he would have failed her so miserably.

He would continue to hope and pray that someday they might be together, but there was no longer a shred of doubt – now wasn't the time.

Paul silently sent up a prayer asking that Trudy would be able to understand that the choice he was making was about protecting her. He hoped she would see that he loved her enough to let her go.

After his morning chores, Paul slept most of Saturday afternoon. He knew he needed to talk to Trudy and inform her of his decision; however, he was unsure as to when he should do it. Should he tell her before the Senior Class Ball or after? It was only a week away.

At first, he surmised that she would want him to take her anyway. But then he decided that was crazy. She would be miserable. Who knew if she would even be willing to speak to him again?

If he waited until after, she might accuse him of leading her on. More than anything he didn't want to do that because it wasn't fair to her. He decided to give himself another day to figure it out. That would mean that if he told her before, she would still have several days to find another date, although he doubted she would.

The thought sent a sharp pain through his heart. He wanted more than anything for Trudy to have that night, even if it wasn't with him. She deserved it. She had never been one to take center stage at her school unless she was actually on stage. He knew that night, with her dressed in a ball gown and her amazing hair done up, she was going to be the most magnificent thing her classmates had ever seen. She would be a princess.

Although it hurt him to think of Trudy with anyone else, he told himself he needed to get used to it. The boys would be lining up the moment they found out that she was free. He hoped he would be able to leave town as soon as school was out so he could spare himself the pain of seeing her hand in hand with another.

CHAPTER TWENTY-FOUR

O n Sunday, Paul awoke to his father yelling up the stairs. "Paul, we have cows out. We've got to go find them before they get in the road and someone gets hurt."

Paul and his father spent the rest of the day tracking down a good portion of their herd. It was late afternoon before they found a break in the west fence line and tracked the cattle almost half a mile from their land.

They were over a tall ridge and down in a large water filled culvert. If it hadn't been for a single "moo," which rang out as they trotted on top of the hill, they would have completely missed them.

By the time they got the herd rounded up and back into their own pasture, it was dark. Hollis stayed at the fence break while sending Paul to get barbed wire to fix it. It was after ten when the duo made it home, shoveled food into their hungry stomachs, cleaned themselves up, and fell into bed.

Paul was almost a walking zombie when he went to school on Monday. His coach got him out of his fifth hour class.

"I want you to stay after practice tonight," he told his pitcher. "There's a scout from St. Louis coming in for tomorrow's game. Paul, I don't know what has been going on with you the last few weeks, but there are only three weeks left in the season. It's now or never."

"I'm going to do this." He looked his coach in the eye. "I know what my problem has been, and I've fixed it. I'll stay as late as you want me to."

Paul went to practice and the coach put him on the mound for the first time in two weeks. Ashton's best batter, Sonny Clay, shared cleanup hitter duties with Paul. His turn at bat usually meant no less than two, and sometimes three runs for the team.

Sonny stepped up to bat. If there was anyone who was going to prove Paul wrong it was Clay, because it was rare that Paul struck him out more than once in a practice.

"Put it in there," his coach nodded to Paul. "Let's see if you're back."

Paul wound up for a Slurve, because Sonny liked to hit outside. In fact if Sonny was thrown a four seam fast ball, it was almost a guaranteed homerun.

Paul looked Jeff in the eye and nodded to him, letting him know he was ready. Then he glared at Sonny, bit his lip and sent the Slurve exactly where it was supposed to go. Paul gasped. It even was faster than he ever remembered throwing before. Sonny jumped out the box and spun.

"Jeepers, Somerton. Where did that come from?" he asked wide eyed.

Paul looked at his coach whose eyes were as wide as Sonny's. Paul saw him mouth the word "Wow," before shaking his head.

"You think you can do that again Son?" he asked.

"Yeah," Paul answered, "I think I can."

"Then do it."

Sonny stepped back into the box a little more hesitant this time. He held up his hand to Paul, signaling that he wasn't yet ready. He kicked the dirt a couple of times before hitting his wooden bat on home plate. It almost looked to Paul like his hard hitting teammate was a little nervous – something Paul had never seen from him before.

Finally Sonny spit, then nodded his head. Paul wound up and sent another Slurve zinging past the plate. The batter swung but it was a full second after the pitch had already passed him.

Sonny's mouth dropped open. "Are you kidding me?" he looked back at Jeff and shrugged his shoulders.

Jeff was shaking his head, as if he also had no answer as to why the best pitcher they had ever known, was now all of the sudden, even better.

"Do it again," the coach yelled.

Sonny looked to the coach as if in protest.

"Do it again!" their leader yelled more forcefully.

Sonny took a deep breath and walked back into the box.

Paul wound up and sent the ball careening over the plate. His teammate jumped from the box again. He looked at his coach and lifted his arms, like he had no idea what had just happened.

"Next batter!" the coach yelled. "The rest of you get out in the field and throw," he ordered.

The rest of the practice was spent with each new batter trying to hit one version or another of Paul's pitches. They weren't successful.

When practice was over, the coach told Paul they were going to go through it all again but he, himself, would be the batter. Paul spent another two hours on the mound.

"How's your shoulder?" the coach asked after they were done.

"It's great," Paul answered. "I'm ready for tomorrow Coach. I'm more ready than I have ever been."

By the time Paul got home, darkness was settling across the land. He rushed through his chores and finally had to resort to lighting a kerosene lantern to finish putting hay and oats in Tillie and Stuart's stalls. He made sure the chickens were up and the coop was secure before heading into the house.

"I tried to keep your dinner warm," his mother apologized "but two hours is a long time. I'm sorry it's cold."

Paul began cramming chicken and dumplings, cornbread, and fried okra in his mouth as fast as he could.

"It's okay, Mom," he managed through his overly stuffed mouth. "Sorry, I'm late. Coach wanted me to stay after practice."

As soon as he finished eating, Paul went to find his father, who was down in the south pasture looking for a lost calf.

Paul could see the lights of his father's old farm truck and followed them.

He came upon his dad, loading the small Herford calf into the back.

"Dad, guess what?" he yelled from about fifteen feet away.

"Come help me Son," he father called back.

Paul ran to the truck and helped his dad lift the crying animal.

"Thank goodness she ain't hurt," Hollis said. "Just somehow got away from her mamma." He closed the tailgate.

"What were you saying?" Hollis turned to look at his son.

"Dad, I pitched better today than I ever have in my entire life. I threw some fast balls that you couldn't even see. Sonny Clay jumped out the box twice against my Slurve," he excitedly relayed.

"That's my boy." Hollis slapped him on the back.

"That's not all," Paul continued. "Tomorrow there's going to be a scout from St. Louis at our game. Dad, if I can pitch tomorrow like I did today, he's going to want me. I know it!" Paul almost couldn't breathe when the reality hit him.

"Son, I have no doubt that you are going to pitch even better tomorrow than you did today. You are always your best under pressure and think about it – you didn't have any pressure today. It was just another practice."

Paul did think about it, and when he did, he shook his head in disbelief. Was it really possible for him to pitch better than he did today? He was sure going to try.

The next morning Paul awoke realizing that he had not talked to Trudy. He had intended on driving the eight miles to her house and speaking with her in person. He owed her that. He vowed that he would do it as soon as he got home from the game.

Paul was surprised at how calm he was going into the game. His coach seemed way more nervous than he was.

"You ready for this?" he had asked Paul, who could see some doubt in his eyes.

"I'm ready Coach. I am." Paul reassured him.

Paul was in fact ready from the moment he stepped on the mound. Ashton was playing the Warren Bulldogs, who were runners up to Ashton in the state finals the previous season. They had all but one starter back this season and they were a force to be reckoned with. Paul and the team never took a game with Warren for granted.

Paul easily struck out the first three batters and closed the first inning three up, three down.

The following eight were more competitive. He allowed one run in the second, third and sixth. He shut them out in the fourth, fifth and seventh and allowed two in the fifth. Ashton scored every inning with at least one and even four runners in the fourth. Ashton's victory was a clean and tidy, thirteen to five.

The score would lead anyone who wasn't at the game to believe that Ashton was just a much better team, but that wasn't the case. Paul carried the victory squarely on his shoulders. Three of Ashton's runs were his. All three times at bat, he managed a triple, making him responsible for five RBI's. On top of his strikeouts, he caught two drives toward second and tagged a runner from third to home. He had the best game of his career, and the team hoisted him onto their shoulders when it was over.

"Paul," he heard his coach holler when he was talking to his dad after the game. Paul turned to see his coach approaching with a man he didn't know.

"Paul, Mr. Somerton," the coach said, nodding to Hollis, "this here is Bruce Benson. He's a scout for the St. Louis Cardinals."

"Mr. Somerton, Paul." Mr. Benson, tipped his hat, "That was a heck of a game you played there Son."

"Thank you sir." Paul smiled. "I appreciate you taking the time to come all the way down here and watch me."

"Oh no," the man answered, "it was all my pleasure, I assure you. Say, would you and your dad mind going to get some supper? I would sure like to visit with you for a little bit."

Paul looked at Hollis, who in turn asked his son if he wanted to go.

"Yes sir, I do Dad."

"Well alright, why don't you get cleaned up and your coach and I will meet you both at that little diner on the highway," the scout said.

"Yes sir, we'll be right there," he answered, as he turned to sprint to the little stone field house where the lockers were located.

"Come over and pick me up Dad!" he yelled back to his father.

Hollis and Paul sat and talked with Bruce Benson and Paul's coach for the next two hours. Paul's future in baseball looked promising.

"We are heavy on pitchers," Bruce told the men, "but several of them are getting on up there. I think at least two of them will be retiring in the next couple of years."

Paul hung on every word the scout said to him, sometimes looking to his dad for confirmation that the man was interested in him.

"You being so young would give us plenty of time to work with you and get you up to speed, but I can tell you that if you continue to play like you did today, I can see you on our mound sooner rather than later."

Paul couldn't believe what he was hearing. It was as if every dream he had ever dreamed about playing professional baseball was coming true at that very moment.

"I want to bring you to camp this summer," Bruce finally said. "I want Billy to see you in person."

"Billy Southworth?" Paul asked in awe.

"That would be the one." Bruce laughed before turning to Paul's father.

"Even if Paul is eighteen, I would still want him to discuss all his decisions with you."

"Paul turned eighteen in October," his father replied.

"No matter," Bruce said returning his gaze to Paul.

"Paul, there's nobody that will look out for you like your family will. Doesn't matter if you are four or forty, you will never go wrong asking your dad for advice. Wish mine was still here so I could." He grimaced at the thought.

"I appreciate that Mr. Benson," Hollis replied. "In that case, why don't you let Paul and me discuss what you are proposing over the next few days, and we will give you call by the weekend. That sound fair?"

"It certainly does," the scout replied, extending his hand to shake Hollis' followed by Paul's.

Benson gave all three men his business card and said his goodbyes. Paul looked at his coach and then his father. The three of them hollered at the same time. Then, they danced around and slapped each other on the back through joyous laughter.

CHAPTER TWENTY-FIVE

Paul and his father both ran into the house as soon as they got home. Imogene was sitting at the kitchen table looking madder than a wet hen.

"Where in the world have you been?! I've been sitting her waiting for you for two hours. I thought you had been in a wreck or hurt!" she seethed. "I've had dinner waiting on you and it's cold and ruined!"

"Aw shucks, Honey," Hollis began to apologize. "I can't believe we forgot to let you know where we were. It's just that you are not..."

Paul jumped in. "Mom, you are not going to believe what happened!"

"You really are not going to believe it Imogene," Hollis interrupted his son.

As Imogene began to calm down, she motioned for them both to sit down.

"Mom, you remember I told you about the scout from St. Louis coming to my game today?" Paul was grinning so big, Imogene could see every tooth in his head.

"Well," Hollis didn't wait for her to answer, "he wants Paul to come to training camp this summer!"

"Can you believe it?!" Paul screamed. "Can you believe it Mom?"

Imogene clapped her hands and got up to hug her only son. She pinched his checks and mimicked Paul's earlier grin as tears slid down her ivory cheeks.

"My baby is going to play for the St. Louis Cardinals." She shook her head trying to take it all in.

"He is," Hollis joined in the hug. "Our boy is headed to the majors."

As soon as Paul arrived at school the next morning he was swarmed by students, as well as teachers, because his coach had already shared the news.

"Congratulations Paul," the bevy of onlookers patted him on the back, shook his hand, and offered praise.

"We knew you could do it," he heard Mr. McIver, his history teacher say.

"You are going to make us so proud," Mrs. Ladner, his English teacher beamed.

The group accolades didn't quit until the first bell sounded. They even followed Paul to his locker, still patting him on the back, before finally releasing him to go to his class.

Paul was floored. He had no idea that people would react that way. He had no idea it meant so much to them too.

He was even more surprised when Mr. Hooper, the principal, announced over the loud speakers that there was going to be a school wide assembly in the auditorium to honor him during last period.

The rest of the day for Paul was a blur. It was filled with even more congratulations, pats on the back and even a few underclassmen asking for his autograph. He was in disbelief.

When the last bell for the final hour sounded, Mr. Hooper again announced that the students should move quickly and quietly to the auditorium. They did with muffled excitement.

Paul saw that, not only were his fellow students in attendance, but also a majority of the town folks. He recognized merchants, the postmaster, farmers, ranchers, retired folks, and the mayor. Just before being called up to the stage by Mr. Hooper, he saw his mom and dad in the front row.

He was humbled beyond belief. Mr. Hooper gave a long speech about the history of great baseball and baseball players who had come from Ashton, Oklahoma, before introducing the school's superintendent, Mr. Ingram.

"Students, esteemed guests," he began "what a great day it is for our school and our community. As you know we are here to recognize, celebrate, and to honor one of our outstanding students."

Paul blushed. He had no idea he would be so embarrassed with the attention.

"Paul Somerton is not only a great baseball player," Mr. Ingram continued, "he is also a great student, a great leader, and a great friend to many of you."

Paul looked at the floor, uncomfortable that he was the center of attention.

"You all know that Paul has been asked to attend the training camp this summer for the ST. LOUIS CARDINALS!" Mr. Ingram yelled, before the entire auditorium jumped to their feet and cheered.

Mr. Ingram held up his hands to quiet them. Paul's face turned crimson.

"Paul," the superintendent turned to look over his shoulder at the man of honor, "you have no idea how proud we all are of you. There is no one who deserves this more. You are one of the finest examples of what a student, a leader, and a friend should be. We know you are going to continue to make us proud, and we want you to know that each and every one of us will be keeping you in our thoughts and prayers, and we will all follow your career for as long as it lasts."

Paul was almost in tears. He could not believe that he was being shown the overwhelming outpouring of love and support. He didn't feel he deserved it, but he was grateful none the less.

"Everyone," Mr. Ingram continued, "welcome our newest Major League Baseball player, Mr. Paul Somerton!"

Again the entire auditorium erupted, everyone stood while students whooped and hollered. The band even played the school song as Paul made his way to the podium.

When the crowd quieted down, Paul stood silently to collect his thoughts. Finally, he cleared his throat, trying to choke back the emotion that was doing everything it could to flood his whole being.

"Thank you all. Thank you so much." He stopped speaking, trying to regain his composure again. "I never thought – I never knew that you all cared so much. I love the game of baseball. I've loved it since I was a tiny boy and my dad would take me into town to watch the peewee league. I couldn't wait to be able to play myself. Once I got on the mound, I never wanted to leave it." Paul's voice began to crack and he lowered his head until he could again breathe. He looked around at all the loving and supportive faces in the auditorium, and again, he choked up.

"We love you Paul," someone in the audience yelled.

Paul smiled. "I love you guys too," a tear slid down his cheek. "I'm just so happy that I've grown up here with all of you. You are the best people in the world." He paused another moment before slapping himself on the forehead.

"Oh my goodness," he laughed, "I need to tell you all something. This may all be a little premature," he laughed again. "You see, just because I'm going to training camp doesn't mean that I will actually be signed to the Cardinals. It's only an opportunity for them to see if they want me." He humbly looked at his feet.

The room was silent for a moment.

"Heck we know that," someone else in the audience yelled.

"We don't care because we know there is no way they will let you go!" another person piped up.

Paul laughed again. "I sure hope you're right. But no matter what, I want you to know how much this means to me. And whether or not I make it, this will always be one of the most special moments of my life."

He looked around the audience again. "Thank you from the bottom of my heart. I promise I will do everything I can to make you proud."

The band bellowed again as everyone jumped and clapped and continued the celebration. Paul stood there, still in disbelief, taking it all in. Townsfolk swarmed the stage, grabbing their chance to throw out a few "Atta boys."

Paul visited with each and every one until the auditorium emptied. Then he and his parents got into their car. Paul smiled all the way home.

T hursday's game was out of town and Paul continued to play the best ball he had ever played. The team did not roll back into Ashton until nearly nine. Paul's father was at the field house waiting for him.

"I took care of your chores," he told his son when he got into the car.

"Thank you so much Pops," the exhausted young man sighed. "I'm not sure I could have made it through. I don't ever remember being this tired."

It must have been true because Paul was asleep by the time Hollis pulled down the long driveway. He woke Paul and sent him up to bed.

Friday morning, Hollis allowed Paul to sleep in and again, took care of his chores. He woke him with just enough time for Paul to get to school.

The congratulations continued throughout the day. Paul thought he must have said "thank you," at least a thousand times in the previous three days. He was grateful that so many people cared.

When school was finally over for the day, Paul headed home. He didn't want his dad to do any more for him. He felt as if he was letting him down by not taking care of his responsibilities.

Paul slopped the hogs and cleaned the horse stalls. He hauled water to the trough, and then noticed that his dad had still not had time to mend a section of fence along their drive. He looked at the sun. He still had plenty of time to get it done and it was the least he could do. He went to the barn and got a bale of barbed wire and a pair of wire cutters before heading down the drive.

Paul had been working on the fence for almost an hour when his dad drove up, stopping where his son was working.

"Getting the fence mended are you?" he smiled at his boy. "I appreciate you taking care of it for me. It's been on my 'to do' list for a good while now."

"I'm happy to do it Dad," Paul smiled back. "I'm just sorry you've had to take up so much slack for me lately."

"It's a small price to pay to have a son who's going to the Big Leagues," he grinned. Paul grinned back.

"You 'bout finished? I bet mom's got supper on the table. Throw that stuff in the back and get in. I'll give you a lift."

Paul threw the wire in the bed and hopped into the cab of the rusty old truck.

"How did your talk go with Trudy?" his dad asked.

Paul's face turned ashen. In all the commotion, he had forgotten to meet with her and tonight was the ball. He looked at his watch. He was supposed to pick her up in ten minutes.

"Dad, I forgot. I forgot!" Paul held his head. "With everything going on, I forgot to go talk to her and tonight is her Senior Class Ball!"

Hollis could see the utter terror in his son's eyes.

"When we get to the house, get the keys to the Buick and get over there. You have to make this right." Hollis sped up the drive like his life depended on it.

Paul jumped from the truck and bounded up the back stairs. He ran to the key rack inside the back door and grabbed the keys to his father's car. Imogene hollered after him.

"Paul, where are you going? Supper is just about ready."

"Dad will tell you Mom, I've got to go!" he yelled back, as he ran out the door.

Paul sped down highway toward Konawa as fast as he could. His stomach was churning. This was not happening the way he had planned.

"How could I have forgotten this?" he asked himself over and over again. *"Trudy is going to hate me. She is going to hate me."* He began to cry, imagining that all they had shared would come to mean nothing to her, and he would never have a chance to marry her if it were to work out.

When he made it to her house, he stopped the car at the end of her driveway. He needed to collect himself – collect his thoughts.

How was he going to tell her everything that he had thought about? How could he possibly make her understand that he was trying to protect her and do what was best of her? When he had made his decision, it all sounded so reasonable. None of it sounded reasonable to him now. He couldn't calm his nerves enough to think straight. His hands were shaking as they sat atop the steering wheel and he felt as if he couldn't get his breath.

He remained there several more moments, trying to form some sort of statement that would make tonight easier for her. He had never felt so pathetic and worthless in his life. How could he have done this to the girl he claimed to love?

Paul saw Knute come to the front door and look down the driveway. He motioned to him to come on up. Paul knew he had to go but he was nowhere close to ready.

Hands still shaking, he put the car in drive and slowly rolled up to the house. When he got out Knute looked him up and down.

"Son, you know tonight is the ball don't you?" he asked, perplexed by Paul's attire.

"Yes sir," Paul meekly answered. "Sir, I need to speak with Trudy."

Knute looked at Paul long and hard. "You want to speak with her?" he asked, as if he hadn't heard the young man correctly.

"Yes sir. Please, may I speak with her?"

Knute continued staring at Paul, not moving. Finally, he turned and opened the door. Paul heard him yell for Trudy.

221

Knute looked back out the doorway at Paul, refusing to look away.

Paul stood motionless, waiting for Trudy to appear. He saw Elsa walk behind Knute and touch his shoulder. Knute turned and Paul saw a look of complete awe cross his face. He was looking at Trudy for the first time. Then Paul saw Knute's face turn to disgust. Elsa saw it too and followed Knute's gaze to the boy on their lawn.

When she saw Paul, still in jeans and an old work shirt, she put her hand to her mouth and gasped. Both she and Knute turned to look toward the daughter that Paul still could not see. Knute motioned for Trudy to come to the door. Paul began to walk toward the house.

With several feet still to go, he saw a flash of blue enter the doorway. He looked up. It was Trudy. She was the most beautiful thing he had ever seen, or ever would see. She literally took his breath away, and it was a full moment before he realized he needed to breathe.

At first he saw a beautiful smile across her face, before she registered what she saw in return. Then the smile began to fade. Trudy stood in confusion, trying to piece together the scene in front of her. She turned to look at Knute and Elsa, who could only return her questioning gaze.

"Paul?" she asked him softly.

He didn't answer.

"Paul?" she said again.

"Trudy, I need to talk to you," he said, taking a step closer.

Trudy too, took a step to the edge of the porch. Knute pushed Elsa back into the house before following himself. They closed the door.

Paul came to the bottom step and looked up at Trudy. She was ravishing. She was beyond any definition of beautiful he had ever known. She was an angel.

"I meant to talk to you sooner," he began. "So much has happened this week. I got a…" he trailed off realizing how empty and pathetic it would all sound.

"Trudy, I love you," he finally managed. "I truly love you but I can't get married right now. It's not fair to you. You deserve better. I can't be there for you. You wouldn't be happy. You would have to give up your dreams. I would have to give up mine. It's not the right time." He tried to build the picture for her that he had built earlier in his own mind, but instead, it was hollow and nothing like what he envisioned it to be.

Trudy began to cry, the definitive words shattering her heart. She felt her stomach plummet like a crashing airplane in a fiery descent.

"Please Trudy, please don't cry," Paul begged the ashen and fragile girl standing before him. "If only you could understand that I'm doing this all for you. I'm trying to make *your* life better. I love you enough to let you go."

Trudy's look of sadness turned to one of confusion and disgust. She swallowed hard and then set her jaw.

"You love me enough to let me go?" Trudy stared at him in disbelief. "You love me enough to let me go?" she repeated, before letting torrents of sobs escape her quivering body.

"It's not coming out right." Paul shook his head. "I need you to know that I love you. Maybe someday we can be together, but I need to play baseball."

"I've never said you couldn't play baseball. I want you to play baseball!" Trudy screamed, before bending over and clutching her stomach as if she was in the worst pain of her life.

Paul moved to her but Trudy pushed him back. She took a deep breath and managed to calm herself before standing back up to face him.

"You can still play baseball and I can go with you." She put her hands on her hips and waited for Paul to agree.

Paul wouldn't look at her, instead he stared at his feet and let silence surround them.

Trudy shook her head.

"I was willing to give up everything for you," she whispered.

"I know Trudy." Paul hesitantly returned her gaze. "I know you were, but you shouldn't. You were meant to be an actress. I was meant to play baseball. It's who we are. It's who we are meant to be. Please, please, try and understand." A tear slipped down his cheek and he stood another moment before wiping his face with the back of his sleeve. Then he turned to look back down the driveway, trying to find the words that so stubbornly refused to emerge.

Finally he looked back at Trudy, who was still looking at him, but shaking her head.

"Why are you doing this to me? Why are you doing this now?" Her face contorted into one of excruciating pain.

Paul tried to take her hand and she recoiled as if he were a snake.

"Just go!" she pointed to the road. "Go! Leave!"

Paul stared at her, struggling within himself, and not knowing what to say in order to help ease her pain.

"GO!" Trudy screamed again. "JUST GO!" She stomped her foot and the poof of marabou bounced up and down. Paul backed away, shaking his head in torment.

"Please," he tried one more time.

Trudy slowly shook her head.

"I love you Trudy," he whispered before turning to get into his car.

Trudy watched the back of the Buick until it was out of sight.

September, 1976

A s she sat at the same farm table where she had grown up, Trudy – who had insisted that she always be called by her "stage name," Doll, beckoned to her elderly mother.

"Ma Ma, why don't we go into the city today? My fans haven't been able to see me for some time."

Elsa's silver hair glowed in the morning sunlight coming through the kitchen window.

"That's a good idea." The fragile woman turned to face her daughter. "I need to stop at the drugstore and have my medications refilled. Maybe we can get some lunch while we are in town too. Would you like that?"

Doll ignored her mother's question.

"You know, the latest Vogue issue says that scarfs are wildly popular. I would like to get one or two. My fans expect me to keep up with the latest fashion trends you know."

"I'm sure we can find some lovely scarfs for you. Since you and Daddy both have birthday's this month, we should stop at the florist too and get some flowers for his grave. We will get a beautiful bouquet for you too." Elsa smiled.

"That will be fine. I just hope I don't have to sign autographs all day. It's so tiresome," Doll yawned. "I'm going to my room to dress."

She arose, retying the belt from her silk robe.

The phone rang and Elsa dried her hands on her apron. She watched Trudy head up the stairs before answering it.

"Hello?" she answered.

It was Judy Walker, one of her closest friends.

"Hello, Judy, it's so nice to hear from you."

Elsa sat down in a small chair next to the phone.

"Actually, today seems to be a good day for her. Trudy – I mean Doll – wants to go into town. I need to stop at the drugstore and I think we might get some lunch. Would you like to join us?"

Elsa twisted the phone cord, trying to untangle it.

"No, I don't think she would mind. Just remember that you must go along with whatever she thinks is going on so she won't get upset."

Elsa stood again, looked around the kitchen door and peered up the staircase. Trudy was nowhere to be seen.

"Okay then, we will meet you at the café at eleven-thirty. See you then."

Elsa hung up the phone before going to the coffee pot, and pouring herself the last cup. She sat down at the kitchen table, knowing Trudy would take more than an hour to get ready.

These days Elsa arose before the sun. She found it hard to sleep with Knute no longer beside her. He had been gone over ten years. He dropped dead of a heart attack while down at their pond, fishing.

At first, Elsa didn't know how she would go on. She found it hard to even get out of bed. Because of Trudy however, she was given no choice, and day by day, the pain lessened until they settled into a new normal.

Although most of Trudy's days were good, sometimes she had a bad spell and there was no consoling her. It was strange.

When Elsa would ask her daughter what had caused her to become so upset, Trudy would have no idea. But Elsa was sure she knew – although she would never have been so cruel as to remind Trudy.

That night, so long ago, when Paul Somerton had broken Trudy's heart, was the beginning of it all. Trudy had come back into the house, she flew past her parents and up to her room. She tore her dress from her body. She threw her shoes across the room. She took her makeup, especially her lipstick and colored all over her face. There were wails of pure agony, as if an animal was being tortured. Elsa and Knute could only watch, because Trudy clawed at them if they tried to come near her.

Elsa saw her rip clumps of hair from her own head. That's when Elsa hit her knees, crying too. Knute's fists were balled, ready to strike out at anything he could, in order to release his own heartbreak. It was pure agony watching his daughter's devastation. It became the worst night of all their lives.

When Trudy had raged until there was nothing left inside her, she took herself to her dressing table. She sat down and looked at herself in the mirror. She took a tissue and began to clean up her face. Running mascara had streaked her cheeks like a zebra, and her bright red rouge and lipstick, appeared clown like. The tissue really only served to smear it more. Elsa got a warm washcloth and gently helped Trudy wash off her skin. She had mostly quietened down, but every so often sniffles erupted.

When Trudy was finally clean, Elsa dressed her in her night clothes and tucked her into bed. It was not even eight but there was sheer exhaustion in her daughter's eye.

Trudy had spent hours getting ready for the ball. First, she and her mother had sat at the kitchen table so Elsa could paint her fingernails for her. Trudy had slept in curlers so that each and every ringlet would be exactly the same when pinned up into a cascade. Trudy had been at her dressing table at least three hours, not only fixing her hair, but also her makeup. The results had been nothing short of stunning.

Only when Knute and Elsa knew that Trudy was asleep, did they dare leave her. They retreated downstairs to the kitchen and Elsa held Knute as he cried like a baby. It was a sight she had never witnessed, not in all the years she had known him. On that night, he let it all out, as if everything he had ever carried inside, could no longer be held back. Elsa's heart was broken – not only for her daughter, but also, for the love of her life. It was something she wouldn't have wished on her own worst enemy.

Elsa sipped her coffee. There was nothing to do now but wait. She had long ago dressed. She wondered, like she had a million times, how differently Trudy's life might have been if it wasn't for Paul Somerton. She didn't blame him. She had forgiven him long ago, realizing that had it been any other girl – although they might have been temporarily heart-broken – they would have eventually managed to pick up the pieces and move on. Looking back, Trudy had exhibited unusual, if not, startling behavior, long before Paul had entered her life.

Elsa and Knute learned that Paul had been chosen to go to training camp that summer with the St. Louis Cardinals. Knute and Hollis had a long talk about everything, and Knute seemed to understand, although he would never understand how Paul could have chosen such a time to break his daughter's heart.

Paul didn't go. He was drafted by the Army right out of school. He was killed in action that fall. Knute and Elsa mourned him in their own way, although they never really remained friends with Hollis and Imogene. Seeing them was just too painful – for everyone involved.

Trudy's parents never told her what had happened to Paul. There was no point. The morning after the ball, Trudy came downstairs for breakfast. She had an exorbitant amount of makeup on. It was not pretty. In fact, it almost bordered on the grotesque. Her lipstick went way beyond her lips, almost touching her nose. She had blue eye shadow up to her eyebrows and large streaks of rouge on her cheeks.

Elsa was taken aback. She looked at Knute, who returned her gaze, but shook his head no, warning Elsa not to say anything about it.

"Good morning Trudy," Elsa said. "Do you want some breakfast?"

Trudy replied in a sultry, husky voice that Elsa had never heard come from her sweet daughter.

"My name is Doll. It's a marvelous stage name."

Knute swallowed hard. Elsa didn't know how to respond. They both sat in silence a few several moments before Knute finally spoke.

"Your stage name?" he asked.

"Of course," Trudy answered. "It's what all my fans know me by."

Knute eyed Elsa again, but neither could find the words to reply.

Trudy ate her breakfast and rose to leave.

"I have a huge performance tonight so I must get my rest." She turned to look at her parents. "Please make sure I'm not disturbed. I'll be in my dressing room."

When she left, Elsa, no longer able to stand, slid into the chair next to Knute's. Her blank stare told him she was as lost to what was happening to their daughter as he was. They sat in silence for what seemed like hours. Knute finally broke it.

"I'm sure it's just a phase. As soon as she feels better – as soon as she realizes that this isn't the end of the world – she will be okay."

Elsa prayed with every fiber of her being that he was correct.

He wasn't.

Even though she was the valedictorian of her class, Trudy never returned to school – not even to graduate. Invitations that had been sent to her from several liberal arts colleges, remained unopened and unanswered, and she never again mentioned Paul. Instead, she immersed herself in "performing" the plays of her past, over, and over, again.

Knute and Elsa's only consolation came from the fact that Trudy was exuberant when she finished each of her "shows." She would stay on the stage her father had built years before, bowing, waving, and smiling to a packed house of invisible fans. She threw kisses and ran from the stage, only to return and take another bow for the encore that only she could hear.

When she finally did leave the stage, she would run into her mother's arms. "Did you see Mother?" she would breathlessly pant. "They adore me!"

Elsa would smile, pat her daughter, and agree. "They do adore you and so do I," she would say with a kiss to her cheek.

Trudy would often take "vacations," which were no more than several days when she would not step onto the stage, but instead would lay in her bedroom reading her latest issue of Vogue, or several different Movie Star magazines. She would tell her mother that she too was going to be interviewed for a cover story. Sometimes she even entertained an invisible reporter in their parlor, answering all sorts of imaginary questions.

The days turned into years and nothing had really changed. Trudy still believed she was young, although she was now about to turn fifty.

The only time Elsa saw a glimpse of the old Trudy, was when Knute died. Trudy wailed, much like she had the night of the ball. She cried all night while lying next to her mother in Elsa and Knute's bed.

"Daddy," she sobbed. "Oh Daddy."

It was as if she had morphed back into the little girl who had wrapped the big, strapping man around her tiny finger. She was never more vulnerable than she had been then. But, as the weeks wore on, Trudy returned to the persona Doll and so it was still.

CHAPTER TWENTY-EIGHT

T rudy returned downstairs. She wore a blue chiffon dress that she had requested her mother buy for her the previous Christmas. It was eerily similar to the one she had chosen for the night of the ball, except for the shade of blue, and of course, the size.

She did have on however, the exact same shoes. She had never given them up, proclaiming them to be divine, and her favorites. She often told others she had gotten them in New York, though Elsa knew better.

"Let's be off, Ma Ma," Doll crooned in her sultry voice. "We can't keep the fans waiting – although I do so tire of them sometimes." She sighed heavily.

Elsa and Trudy headed into town and stopped at Stephen's Drugstore first.

Most people in town were aware of Trudy's condition, and they were kind enough to go along with her fantasy. Elsa had a deep appreciation for the town and its people. It seemed to have more than its share of eccentrics, but the townsfolk all seemed to take care of them. With Trudy being one of them, Elsa felt blessed that this had been the place they had settled.

Trudy swept into the store, cigarette stylus in hand – although she didn't smoke. She had insisted that her mother buy her one after she saw another star with one on the cover of one of her Hollywood magazines.

Trudy entered the store, dramatically throwing an arm into the air, as if announcing her arrival on a great stage. She then stopped in her tracks, almost causing her mother to bump into her. She then scanned the store. Elsa waited patiently behind her daughter, knowing what was coming.

Trudy began waving – just like Miss America – to the almost empty store. She had adopted the wave many years earlier after she and her mother watched the pageant.

Elsa bit her lower lip, hoping that anyone who was in the store was aware of her daughter's condition. She watched from behind as Trudy acknowledged the imaginary crowds that awaited her. It wasn't long before Trudy grew tired of the admiration however, and stopped it, by loudly announcing

"Enough!" and telling the invisible crowd that she just wanted some peace.

Then she turned and escorted her mother through the door and up to the store's soda fountain.

"Ma Ma," she crooned in her sultry voice, "Please order me a Coca-Cola. Oh, and have them add some cherry."

Unless she was addressing her fans, Trudy had long ago stopped speaking to the "common folk," as she liked to call them. Instead, she used her mother as her voice.

Elsa started to relay the message but saw that the teenaged girl behind the soda fountain, was already fulfilling the request. The pretty little girl was the daughter of the store's owner and she almost reminded her of Trudy when she was that age. She silently wondered how this young lady's life would turn out. She envied Mary Ann, the pharmacist, and the girl's mother, for she could still dream about what wonderful things her daughter might accomplish in life. Elsa's time to do that had long ago passed, and the dreams she had for Trudy couldn't have been further than the reality in which she was living.

Elsa surmised that the girl – Olivia she thought was her name – must have been raised right because, with the exception of the first time she had seen Trudy, she had been going along with Trudy's fantasy. She sighed to herself, remembering their first encounter.

It had been at least five years earlier. The teen was still just a child. When she and Trudy had entered the store, the girl had stared at Trudy, wide eyed and bewildered. It had been the same with almost everyone who didn't know Trudy's story.

One of the store's older clerks, Alberta, had moved the child out of the way and took over Trudy's order. Luckily, Trudy hadn't noticed the somewhat nervous stares of the girl.

At first Elsa was upset and defensive. She glared at the girl, but when she got ahold of herself, she felt ashamed. It was a perfectly normal reaction, especially for a child. She was always kind to the young lady now though. In fact, she was even grateful. How many young people would play along with such a farce? Elsa figured it was one of the reasons Trudy felt comfortable going to the drugstore and usually came along when Elsa had to go.

"Right Away Miss Dahl," the girl said, interrupting Elsa's day dreaming. "How are you today?" she asked Trudy, who turned to her mother.

"Ma Ma," Trudy began, "Tell her I am well."

Before Elsa could relay the message the girl replied.

"That is just lovely, and so are you today Doll. Your dress is spectacular."

Elsa watched Trudy tilt her nose into the air, before she ordered her to pay for the soda. Then she escorted Trudy to the first of four soda tables which were located directly past the fountain.

"I'm going to fill my prescriptions dear. Will you wait on me here?"

Trudy swished the dingy, white feather boa – the same one she had worn that fateful night – behind her neck before brushing off the metal soda chair, and sitting down to sip her cola.

Trudy saw there were more fans at the remaining tables, waiting for her. She hoped they would let her drink her soda in peace. *"Everyone wants so much from me,"* she thought to herself. She sometimes felt it was too much, especially when a girl just needed her space.

"Beautiful Day Miss Dahl," an older gentleman said to her. He acted as if he knew her personally, then he tipped his ball cap like it was a top hat. Doll was not impressed.

"My, aren't you pretty today," another man chimed in.

"Just like a picture," a third added.

She tried to ignore them. Didn't they see that she just wanted to be by herself?

"Happy to see you in town today," a large gray-haired man boomed, startling her.

"Peasants," she hissed under her breath.

Trudy had enough of the continuous adoration. She arose from her seat and sauntered over to a display of greeting cards. Maybe they would get the hint and let her be, she thought to herself.

She fingered several of the cards, looking at the pictures on the front. One had a big monkey that was wearing bright red lipstick. She smiled a little before taking a long drag from her stylus, and blowing fake smoke out her puckered lips.

There was also a card with an ocean and a sunset. It was very pretty. It reminded her of the time she appeared on tour with Bob Hope, to entertain the troops in Hawaii.

Then she spied another card with a large foil heart. It floated atop a bride and groom. She felt a tear come to her eye, but she had no idea why. She pulled a little lace handkerchief –

that her daddy had given her – from her bosom, and dabbed her eyes. She felt an overwhelming sadness fill her heart. Her eyes began to flutter and she felt as though she might faint. The uncomfortable feeling sent her into somewhat of a panic and she yelled to her mother.

"Go! I want to go!" she looked toward the pharmacy area at the back of the store. Unable to see her mother, her panic began to rise.

"I said I want to go!" She stomped her feet harshly. It was then she could finally see Elsa rise from a bench near the back register. The older woman ran to her daughter's side.

"Oh my," she said, quickly steering her daughter away from the cards. Elsa looked at the four men seated at the soda tables and with her eyes, apologized for the outburst.

We'll go right now," she whispered, hugging Trudy close to her.

Elsa led Trudy from the store, relaying over her shoulder to the young woman behind the fountain that she would return later for her prescriptions. Then she loaded her child into their car.

When Elsa herself got inside and was situated, she turned to her daughter.

"Are you okay dear?" she softly asked.

Trudy dabbed her eyes again and sniffled. She sat in silence a moment longer before taking a deep breath.

"It's just so hard to have so many people who want my attention," she finally answered. "Sometimes a girl just needs to have her own time. I can't go anywhere without being swarmed."

Elsa exhaled and then patted the woman-child's knee.

"I know, Dear. I'm so sorry. Maybe we can try again next week. Hopefully there won't be so many of your fans in town."

"Yes, that's a good idea," Trudy nodded her head in agreement. "We will come back when there aren't so many of my fans around."

Elsa drove home and when she parked the car, Trudy jumped out and rushed upstairs to her room. Elsa silently watched her ascend the porch stairs. She sat a moment longer, trying to mentally prepare herself in case Trudy's day had been ruined. She finally got out of the car, and went to the kitchen.

Elsa filled the kettle and put it on the stove. She hoped some tea might help calm her nerves. She remembered the lunch she had planned with her friend Judy. She walked to the phone, called and canceled, apologizing, but promising a raincheck. Then she made herself a cup of Earl Grey and sat down at the table. It wasn't long before Trudy returned to the kitchen.

"I have a matinee to do today," she gleefully informed Elsa.

Elsa smiled with relief.

"I will see you after the show." Trudy giggled and bent over to give her mother a peck on the cheek.

Elsa looked adoringly at her only child. "I'll be along in a moment. Break a leg, Sweetheart."

Elsa still watched every performance that Trudy gave. It was in those times that even through the fog of Trudy's mind, she could glimpse her real child – the child that might have been. It also gave her a chance to pretend too – to pretend that her baby had grown up to see all her deepest desires come to fruition.

Elsa looked at her withered hands, then she turned her focus back to Trudy. She dreaded the day that would come, when Trudy would no longer get to play to an audience of one.

"Best to stay in the here and now," she told herself.

For in the here and now, Trudy was happy.

ACKNOWLEDGEMENTS

First I want to thank my mother-in-law Barbara Shelton, whose great-grandparents, Anders Fjelland and Ragnhild Apeland Fjelland immigrated to the United States from Norway. After arriving with their church congregation in Lisbon, Illinois, they found there was no land to be had, so they moved to Story County, Iowa, settling there permanently.

It is from my mother-in-law that I learned the fascinating history of the Norwegian settlers in Iowa. I am lucky that her Norwegian roots run deeply, as I have been privileged to experience some of the fantastic Norwegian cuisine mentioned in this story. Especially during holidays, our family gets to feast on her famous Sour Cream and Raisin pies. In addition, many bakeries around the settlement areas still sell the pastry Kringla. If you ever get a chance to try it, you must.

To my very good friend, and legendary Oklahoma independent oil and gas producer, Mike Cantrell, I want to thank you for all the information about life on an oil rig. Mike started his career the same as Knute. His success in the oil business has led him to be one of the most respected men in the industry and a champion of independent producers.

I would also like to thank my amazing first readers and editors, Carol Cervi McCurdy and Barbara DePrater Gregory. I truly appreciate your keen eyes and suggestions. I'm so thankful that you both take the time to help make my books the best they can be.

Finally to my incredibly talented and beautiful daughter, Brealyn Elizabeth Wren for the cover art. You continue to amaze me with your talent and the way you understand my vision. I couldn't do it without you.

And once again to all my readers, I am humbled by your continued support. Because of you, I am blessed.

ABOUT THE AUTHOR

SD Shelton is the award-winning and best-selling author of the memoir *Me, the Crazy Woman, and Breast Cancer.* She is also the author of *The Drugstore Series* and is a multi-award-winning former broadcast and print journalist.

On any given Saturday during football season, you will find her hanging out with her best friends, watching University of Oklahoma Football and yelling "Boomer Sooner" a lot.

She lives in Oklahoma and has an intense fondness for her three dogs. There's the old man, Teddy, "Theodore the Lionhearted," a compilation of Chow and Golden Retriever; and two barky, rambunctious Miniature Schnauzers, Walter Roux and Harvard Winslow. Wally and Harvey were born in Konawa and have their own following on Facebook under #BiteyBabies.

Starring Doll Dahl is the fourth book of eight in *The Drugstore Series.* Watch for the fifth installment, *The Tinsleys*, coming Spring of 2019.

Connect with SD on Facebook @SDSheltonBooks